A Relic to Die For

RICHARD HOUSTON

Version 2017.12.24

Cover Art by Victorine Lieske

ISBN-13: 978-1973942139

ISBN-10: 1973942135

To Samantha

ACKNOWLEDGMENTS

The author could not have finished this book without the help of his editors and beta readers:

Elise Abram, www.eliseabram.com

Victorine Lieske, www.bluevalleyauthorservices.com

RICHARD HOUSTON

Chapter 1

Fred followed me like a blind puppy. He was bound to bruise his nose if I made a sudden stop. Fred is neither a puppy nor is he blind. Like me, he was scared. I didn't believe in zombies or ghosts, and I'd be willing to bet my next paycheck—if I ever get a next paycheck—that Fred didn't either. Still, I couldn't get them out of my mind as we crept through the abandoned cemetery, looking for Captain Howard Scott's grave. The urge to give it up and go home was overruled by the need to pay my bills and feed a dog who ate more than I did.

I'd been hired by Margot Scott to find the Captain's grave and see if it had been robbed. Margot was the wife of the Captain's great, great grandson, and the twin sister of my good friend and neighbor, Bonnie Jones. Margot's son had seen a Confederate officer's sword for sale on eBay with the family name inscribed on it. The listing was deleted when he sent an email asking the seller how he got the sword, but not before he managed to download pictures of it. When he showed them to Margot, she recognized it as the sword of her husband's great, great-grandfather from an ancient tintype. She remembered stories of how he had been buried in full uniform, along with his sword, on the family homestead in Southern Missouri. The current owner of the farm refused to let the sheriff on his property without a warrant, so I was hired to do the job.

We had looked at a dozen headstones when Fred left my heels to check out a small grave with a weathered stone. Although the moon was nearly full, a cloud chose the moment to block its light. I used my flashlight to read the weather-worn epitaph: "*God needed a special angel. One loving and kind. And so He chose our child. And left us all behind.*" I couldn't read anymore and bent down to hug Fred around the neck.

I knew dogs have excellent night vision, but there was no way he could have known the grave was that of a child—dogs can't read. I wiped my eyes and whispered, even though the nearest house was over two hundred yards away, "You need glasses, Freddie. Sarah isn't even close to Howard."

Fred raised his head and pointed in the direction of the adjacent grave. I didn't need my flashlight to read the name. The weather-worn stone was barely legible. I couldn't read the epitaph, but the name,

Howard Scott, had been carved deeply enough to last 150 years of Missouri ice and wind. I patted Fred on the head and got up to inspect the Captain's last resting place.

The dirt around his grave was covered with the same wild grass and weeds as all the others and didn't look like it had been disturbed. There was even a small cedar tree of five or six feet that had taken root in the center of his grave. The tree was at least three or four years old. I suppose Howard's grave could have been dug up before the tree took root, but why would the grave robber wait so long to sell his loot? It was a question I wouldn't have time to ponder.

Fred started to growl, looking toward the farmhouse. I turned to look and froze. Several exterior floodlights had the yard lit up like a high school football field. The light beams didn't reach us, but it wouldn't be long before the light of a powerful flashlight coming toward us did. I turned off my flashlight and headed for the road, praying we could get to a small shack a few yards beyond the fence of the cemetery before the farmer could see us. The old shed should shield us from any gunshot long enough for us to reach Bonnie's Jeep and escape. I was just yards from the fence when I felt the ground disappear beneath my feet. A second later, I landed flat on my back, knocking the air out of my lungs.

The hole I hadn't seen wasn't more than five or six feet deep—that I could estimate from Fred's presence at the top of the pit. He stood at the rim barking for me to get my fat butt up before the farmer could catch us, or at least that's what I thought he was trying to tell me. For all I knew, he could have been laughing his head off.

My flashlight had gone flying when I'd fallen. The light from the moon was no help in the darkness of the hole, so I felt around for my flashlight, and my hand bumped up against a soft object in the process. I didn't need light from the moon or otherwise to tell me it was a body. I'm sure if the Olympics had a jumping out of a pit event, I would win gold. I was out of the hole and over the cemetery fence in record time. We didn't stop for breath until we were within sight of Bonnie's Jeep, with only the shed between us and the cemetery. A second later, we heard a gunshot. I still didn't believe in zombies—despite my encounter with what must have been a corpse, so it had to be the farmer. He let loose five or six rounds in rapid succession. Less than a minute later we were in the Jeep, spraying gravel from all four wheels.

Chapter 2

The ride back to our motel gave me more than enough time to second guess my decision to let Margot hire me. I must have been temporarily insane when I agreed to drive out to Truman, Missouri and check on her husband's family cemetery. It seems like every time I try to help Bonnie, we get caught up in a murder. Then again, maybe I was letting my paranoia get the best of me. The corpse I'd fallen on could have been dug up by grave robbers and not murdered at all. Still, I couldn't stop thinking of some of our past experiences.

Along with Fred, it seems Bonnie and I have been involved in more murders than Jessica Fletcher, or Father Brown. Like them, we're not exactly professionals but have somehow managed to get involved in deadly crimes that we had to solve. More than once it was because one of us was the suspect. Solving murders was the only thing we had in common with those sleuths. Bonnie's a good twenty-five years older than me, and Fred is a dog.

Margot's recent bypass has kept Bonnie a slave to her twin, making it impossible for her to join us, but she did lend us her Jeep. My old Wagoneer was on its last legs. It drank faster than an AA member falling off the wagon and went through oil almost as fast. It wasn't up to a 750-mile trip, so Bonnie insisted I take her Jeep, making me promise to keep her in the loop with whatever I found.

I wanted to call her once Fred and I were back at the safety of our motel but waited until a decent hour. It was barely dawn when we got back, and Missouri is an hour ahead of Colorado, so I watched the news on TV while waiting for a decent hour to call. I'd barely started brewing coffee in the motel's coffee maker when my cell rang. I hit the TV's mute button when I saw it was Bonnie.

"You're up early, Jake. Did Fred wake you?"

"No, Bon. He's still sleeping after being up half the night. We only got back from Sleepy Hollow a few hours ago and I couldn't sleep after the headless horseman took a pot shot at us. Evidently, it didn't bother Fred."

"Someone shot at you? Are you guys okay?" I could see her reaction in my mind's eye. Her only daughter had been killed in a car accident years ago, and her husband died shortly afterward. Over time, she'd come to think of Fred and me as her children. She must have been horrified to think she'd put us in harm's way.

"We're fine. I wish I could say the same for the body we found, but other than a couple new gray hairs, we're okay."

"You found a body? Was it decapitated?" This time my mind painted a picture of Bonnie with her mouth open and her cloudy gray eyes the size of small planets.

"Why would you think that, Bon?"

"Your reference to Sleepy Hollow—I assumed that's why you brought it up."

"Oh, sorry about that. No, the corpse still had his head… I think. I was in such a hurry to get out of there I didn't have time to check. But that's not why I called. I thought Margot might like an update on Captain Scott's grave."

"You found the grave?"

"Yes, and it's my guess the sword wasn't buried with him. Either that or the grave had been robbed a long, long time ago. There's even a cedar tree growing in it."

"Those are like weeds in Missouri, Jake. It's probably less than a year old. And why did you guys choose the middle of the night to check it out anyway?"

"It's a long story, Bon."

"I'm listening. Margot won't be up for at least another hour, and her fancy coffee pot takes forever, so go ahead and tell me."

Mention of the coffee pot reminded me to pour myself a cup with my free hand. It also brought back memories of all the mornings Fred and I would walk down to her place for coffee. We lived on a dirt road in the hills outside of Denver. Her house was just below our cabin. More often than not, she'd fix breakfast for us, and Fred would end up with the lion's share. I took a sip of coffee before starting the story of the previous night's adventure, and spit it back out, gagging.

"Are you okay, Jake?"

"Sorry, Bon. It's the coffee. It tastes like sewer water. I sure miss yours."

My outburst woke Fred, who'd been sleeping at my feet, to wake up. His ears rose at the mention of Bonnie's name, not in the stiff and focused way a Shepherd or Pincher does, but he did a good imitation, considering he's a Golden Retriever. "By the way, Bon, Fred says hi."

"Hi, Fred!" she yelled, nearly bursting my eardrum. "Would you tell your master to quit stalling and get on with it?"

I rubbed my ear before continuing. "Okay, but

remember you asked for it." I paused long enough for a dramatic effect, but not long enough for her to respond. "To answer your first question, we were there in the middle of the night because the guy who now owns the farm, Mathew Cramer, according to the mailbox, wouldn't give me permission to check out the cemetery when I'd asked him the day before."

"I already know who owns the farm, Jake. Tell me something I can give to Margot." I ignored her sarcasm. She must have got out the wrong side of the bed.

"Yes, ma'am. Cramer must have heard us snooping around. My back was turned toward the farmhouse and we probably would have been caught if Fred hadn't seen him coming toward us. We were almost home safe when I fell into an open grave. That's when I found the body. I wasn't in the hole long, but it was long enough for Cramer to get close enough to shoot at us."

I expected a "What?" but all I got was silence. "You still there, Bon?" I prayed I hadn't given her a heart attack.

"Are you all right? What about Fred?"

"No... I mean yes. Fred's fine, but I'm not so sure about me." Fred must have lost interest in the voice on the other end of the phone and went back to sleep. I considered taking another sip of coffee but decided it could wait.

"Do you need a doctor?"

"Maybe a psychiatrist. I seem to find trouble without trying, or maybe it finds me."

Bonnie replied with something between a laugh and a snicker before answering. "I knew I should have come with you. I can't leave the two of you alone for a minute before you're in trouble. But at least you found out who stole Captain Scott's sword."

"How do you figure, Bon?" I kept my own snicker in check. I didn't want to make her feel bad, but I had to wonder how she jumped to that conclusion.

"The dead guy was robbing graves and Cramer caught him and shot him. Find out who he is and you'll find the sword."

It wasn't the time to mention I'd been too scared to even think of looking at the corpse. "I didn't have time to check the corpse for bullet wounds. You're probably right about Cramer shooting him, but not because he was caught robbing graves. It's probably Cramer digging up the artifacts and who shot the guy for trespassing at the crime scene. Either that or Cramer and the stiff were in it together and something went wrong. Are you forgetting Captain Scott's grave wasn't dug up? Margot will be wasting a lot of money having me follow up on a dead man."

"Does that mean you won't try to find out who he is?"

"Not at all. I'll see if he has a wallet or something when I go back to fetch my flashlight. I only meant I'd be wasting time because the trail to the Captain's sword lies somewhere else."

"You left your flashlight in his grave?" I didn't need Skype to imagine her mouth falling open.

"It's why I have to go back. If the police find it, they'll think *I* murdered him."

There was another long pause before she continued. I had no idea if she was doing the happy dance or silently cussing at me. I suspected the later until I heard her talking to someone else. I didn't need the help of Johnny Carson's Carnac the Magnificent to know it was Margot. They were arguing about something, so I decided to try my coffee once more while waiting. I'm addicted to the stuff. Even if it's made with sewer water, I have to have a cup. I'd barely had a swallow when Bonnie came back online. "Jake, Margot agrees with you, so I guess I'm outvoted."

"Margot agrees with me? That's got to be a first."

"She said you should be concentrating on what she paid you to do and not get involved in another murder."

I knew there had to be a catch. Margot and I never agreed on anything. "Good enough. I'll call the sheriff's office and leave an anonymous message about the body after I get my flashlight back. With luck, Cramer will be arrested, and I'll have all the time in the world to check Margot's grave in the daylight."

"You mean Captain Scott's grave; Margot isn't dead yet."

"We should be so lucky."

"Jake! She can hear you."

"Just kidding, Bonnie. You know I love her like a sister." What she didn't know is my sister and I fought like Siamese fighting fish when we were kids.

"Just the same, it's nothing to kid about."

"Tell Margot not to worry about me wasting her money. Once I get my flashlight back, I'll do some online snooping to see if I can't find the guy who was selling the sword on eBay while we wait for the sheriff to arrest Cramer. And if that doesn't put him in jail, I'll find a way to get him off the farm long enough to do a proper search."

Another pause while Bonnie repeated what I'd said. "She likes how you think, Jake. Call me back later tonight and let us know how it's going. And make sure Fred gets some good food."

Fred raised his head as I said goodbye and

disconnected the call. "Don't tell me you understood that," I said, leaning down to rub his head. In the process, I happened to glance up at the TV, which was still muted. I didn't need sound to tell that the farm in the picture with a Fremont County Corner's van belonged to none other than Mathew Cramer.

Chapter 3

I remembered the Springfield news anchor from the last time I'd been in Truman. She had the perfect Midwestern accent, and never once stuttered or said words like "uh", but I doubt she'd make it past the mailroom back in Denver. She simply wasn't skinny enough or young enough for that market. I thought she was exactly the kind of woman I'd love to meet, but then I'm pushing fifty, and Denver's age demographic is much younger. I'd missed most of the broadcast but did manage to hear enough to forget about making the anonymous call to the sheriff's office.

"Mrs. Crouch doesn't have any idea who could have killed him in such a terrible manner. She says he was the kind of person who would give his last dollar to a vet or homeless person on the freeway off-ramp. This is Carla Kennedy. Back to you, Rick."

Any hope Rick would clarify Carla's remarks were drowned out by a series of commercials. Who was this Mrs. Crouch? And why didn't Carla interview Cramer instead? Then it hit me. I could really be dense sometimes. The sheriff must have arrested Cramer, and Mrs. Crouch must have known the dead guy I'd fallen on. Why else would she have such kind words for him? He was probably her husband or boyfriend. More importantly, *had they found my flashlight?*

I shut off the TV when a commercial of a car dealer giving away a rifle with every new truck purchase told me the news was over, and quickly booted my laptop to see if the TV station had posted the interview on its web page. Still nothing. Whatever WiFi service the motel claimed to have wasn't working. That left my smartphone. I rarely used it to web surf because my plan had such low data limits, but I convinced myself this was a business expense I could charge to Margot. Again nothing, not a single bar. I couldn't get a single bar. Calling the TV station to ask if Carla had mentioned a flashlight next to the body in the grave wasn't an option. Even asking who the stiff was and how he'd been killed was too risky. I'm sure they record, or at least log, all calls. I didn't need to put myself on any suspect list, if I wasn't already. I really needed a cup of coffee if I were going to come up with a viable plan, so I refilled my cup and sat down in the only chair in the motel room to think.

The view from the chair was almost as bad as the coffee. In the ten minutes or so I sat staring out the window trying to think, I counted two pickups pulling boats headed for the lake, and a school bus. Other than that, all I had to look at was an empty parking lot and some deserted buildings across the street. I remembered that one had been an ice cream shop from my last visit, but couldn't recall what the others had been. Evidently, they never recovered from the recession.

"Could this be what drove that stiff to rob graves?" I said aloud.

Fred woke again at the sound of my voice and stared at me.

"Speaking of the stiff, Fred, do you think Cramer shot him like Bonnie said?"

This time he wagged his tail.

Then it hit me. "Damn it, Fred!"

My tone of voice made him stop wagging his tail, and put it between his legs. "He's probably telling them right now that I killed the guy in the grave. We've got to get that flashlight back if it's still there."

Fred didn't answer, but got up and went to the door.

"Lie back down, Freddie. We need a plan before

we go off half-cocked."

He ignored me and began scratching at the door.

"Okay, Freddie, I don't know what made me think you understood me, but stop that or you'll get us kicked out of here." The motel wasn't exactly pet-friendly, but it was nearly as empty as the stores across the street when we checked in. With a little persuasion and a hundred dollar, non-refundable deposit, I'd convinced the manager to rent us a room. That might change if she thought Fred was destroying the place.

Fred stopped scratching and turned toward me, smiling. I couldn't tell if his smile was because he got my attention. Goldens are always smiling. "Can you wait until I put on some pants? I don't think the manager would appreciate me walking you in my skivvies."

Fred answered with a bark.

Our little walk around the motel to find the proper tree for Fred failed to inspire any great ideas on how to get my flashlight back if, it was still there. For all I knew, it could be stored away in the county evidence room as Exhibit A for an upcoming murder trial. I needed to see the video of that interview, which meant I had to find an Internet connection. I knew, from my last visit, that Truman had a nice library with free WiFi, but I also knew the local McDonald's did, too, and better yet they had decent coffee.

Fred recognized his favorite restaurant the minute I pulled in. I reached over and rubbed his ears before going inside. "Promise you'll behave yourself while I watch the video and I'll buy you a couple McDoubles."

I swear I saw his eyes light up. I hadn't given him any fast food since Julie, my second wife, died a few years ago. She'd insisted it wasn't good for him and made me promise to stop. I quit petting Fred and looked up to the heavens. Well, it would have been the heavens if we weren't sitting in Bonnie's Jeep, but I'm sure Julie got the idea. "I'll order it without onions or pickles, Honey. In fact, I'll just give him the meat, okay?" When I wasn't struck by lightning or a tornado, I assumed she had no objections, so I lowered Fred's window and went inside. The window wasn't necessary as the chance of Fred succumbing to heat exhaustion in the first week of March was nil, but he liked it cold.

After ordering a large black coffee, I found a long bench seat where I could sit with my back to the wall. It made me think of something Doc Holliday once said about sitting where nobody could sneak up on him. Only in my case it wasn't to avoid being shot in the back, but so no one could watch over my shoulder. Unfortunately, I was too close to the television. At first it didn't bother me much. I thought they might switch to local news and I'd be able to catch a replay of the story I'd missed earlier. No such luck. The TV was tuned to a Fox cable station that wouldn't stop talking about Trump and Hillary. The election was eight months away, and all they could talk about was politics? I finally gave up on TV and connected my phone to McDee's WiFi.

It took me less than five minutes to find what I needed. The Springfield station had posted the video of Carla Kennedy at Cramer's farm. My luck was changing, or so I thought. I'd left my earbuds back in the motel, and for some strange reason the place was filling up with a bunch of gray-haired people. There was no way I could play the video without bringing attention to myself. When an older couple approached looking for a place to sit, I had no choice but to close my phone and move over. They were both wearing bright-red caps with the words, "Make America Great Again" on them. He had worn-out Levis and a flannel shirt that had seen one too many washes. His wife's cotton dress wasn't in much better shape.

The husband looked grateful and offered his

hand. "Thank you, son. Are you here to play Bingo, too? I don't think I've seen you before."

"No, sir. I just came in to use the Internet," I said, nodding toward my phone.

His wife spoke before he could answer. "Well, don't let us stop you. There's plenty of room at this table for all of us." She was right. The table could easily seat eight people. It had four chairs in front and a long bench seat against the wall.

The old guy waited for his wife to finish before speaking again. "Thank you, son. I promise we'll be as quiet as a church mouse."

I forced a smile and went back to my phone. I was dying to read the text I'd seen accompanying Carla's video.

"Isn't he such a sweet boy, John. Make sure you get an extra Egg McMuffin when you order," she said to her husband before turning her attention to me. "My name's Ella, by the way, and that old geezer is my husband, John. You will join us, I hope?"

I hesitated long enough for her smile to droop. I'd forgotten I couldn't order Fred his McDoubles this early in the morning and was wondering how he'd like a couple McMuffins instead. "Sorry, ma'am, I was thinking about something else. Thanks, but I've already eaten." Sometimes telling the truth hurts. I had to lie so I didn't hurt their feelings. I couldn't tell them that I didn't think they could afford to buy me breakfast.

I went back to reading Carla's article while John went up to order. At least I thought I'd be able to read it. John wasn't gone a minute when Ella spoke up. "I sure hope he wins, don't you?"

"Huh?" I answered, looking up from my phone.

"Trump. Don't you think he'll be a great president?"

That's when I noticed she was watching the TV. The last thing I needed, was to get into a discussion about politics. I'd learned long ago it was useless to voice my opinion unless I wanted to spend the next hour defending it.

"Do you own a gun?" she asked.

"Just a shotgun my father left me. I'm not really into hunting."

"Well, be prepared to turn it in if she wins. As if that would stop people from killing each other. They'll keep killing each other whether they have guns or not, like poor Mr. Cramer last night."

I nearly dropped my phone into my coffee. "Cramer was murdered?" I hoped she hadn't seen the shock on my face.

She pushed her glasses closer to her eyes and leaned forward in her chair. "You know him?"

I had to think quickly. The tone of her voice

suggested she had taken the defensive. "My grandparents used to live around here and had a neighbor by that name, or maybe he was just a friend. I only got the information second hand, but tell me about it. What happened?"

"It was all over the news this morning. His daughter couldn't get him on the phone and when she went to check on him, found him hanging in his barn."

"In the barn? He killed himself?"

Ella's eyes narrowed, exposing deep grooves. "Not likely. Not unless he had zombie powers."

"What?"

"How could you not know about zombies? Don't you watch TV?"

"I know what a zombie is, but I never watch those shows. I was wondering why you thought he had superhuman powers."

The corners of her mouth began to form a little smile. "Because nobody knows how he got up there. Someone had to take the ladder, or whatever they used, with them."

"Oh. Do they have any idea who did it?"

Suddenly, the room quieted down and the old lady turned her attention to her Bingo cards. Someone at another table had the floor. It was the Bingo lady who could have been Ella's twin. "I-twenty-three," she called out.

Fred's tail was doing a great imitation of an unbalanced ceiling fan when I returned to the car. It stopped when he saw I didn't have his treat. "Sorry, boy. They won't be serving McDoubles for another hour or so," I said as I got into the Jeep.

He moved over to the passenger seat, laid his head between his paws and stared at me. "How about I go through the drive-thru after I finish reading about old man Cramer? Will you settle for an Egg McMuffin instead?" He answered with a wimp thump of his tail while I turned my attention back to my cell phone.

This time, I was able to listen to the video. The only eavesdropper was Fred and something told me he was more concerned with breakfast than the video. Not that it mattered. There was no mention of the corpse in the grave or my flashlight. It did confirm what Ella had told me about Cramer's daughter finding his body hanging in the barn, but not a peep about the other corpse. It was beginning to look like another trip to the farm was the only way I could tell for sure if my flashlight was still there. I no sooner closed the web browser when my phone rang and startled me. A quick glance told me it was Bonnie again.

"Jake? Boy, am I glad I got you before the cops did."

I felt my blood pressure rise significantly. "Cops? Why would they be after me?"

Her voice suggested I wasn't the only one with high blood pressure. "Someone got your—I mean, my—license number when you sped away from Cramer's farm. They called me to see if my Jeep had been stolen."

I knew she meant the cops called her and not the person who reported it, but I let it slide.

"What'd you tell them?"

"I thought about saying it was stolen, but if they found you before you could ditch it, you'd be in deeper than you are now, so I told them the truth."

"You told them about the body?"

"No, Jake. I said I lent you my Jeep so you could take care of some business for Margot back in Missouri. I hope I didn't get you in any trouble."

I was about to answer when two State Trooper SUVs and a local police car pulled in. "I'll have to call you back later, Bon. The posse just showed up."

I turned my attention to Fred, wondering who would take care of him while I was locked up waiting for Bonnie to bail me out. "Looks like breakfast is going to be at the local jail, Freddie."

Fred sensed my worried tone of voice and put

his head on the fold-down armrest separating the two front seats. I glanced at him and then focused on my rearview mirror, waiting for them to surround the Jeep. To my amazement, the three cruisers drove on and around toward the back of the parking lot. My first instinct was to start the Jeep and drive away, but to do so would mean I'd have to drive around the restaurant and past the cops. That would be stupid. My out of state plates were bound to be noticed, and for all I knew they could be running a check on them as I sat in the Jeep wondering what to do. I didn't have long to wonder.

As I watched through the glass windows of the restaurant, I saw the cops park their cars and enter through the back door. I crossed myself and said a silent Hail Mary when they all went to the counter to place their orders.

Chapter 4

Fred looked disappointed as I drove past the drive-thru and around the restaurant. I didn't want to risk waiting in line for Fred's sandwich and hoped the cops would be too busy ordering to notice me leaving. He didn't seem any happier when I promised to get him his plain McDoubles on the return trip, but first we needed to see if the sheriff was still at the farm.

I avoided the farm and approached the cemetery from the south. When I didn't see any other vehicles on the road I parked in nearly the same place as the night before. The cemetery was nearly as spooky during the daylight as when I'd stumbled on the corpse the night before. The only trees with leaves were some skinny cedars. All the hardwoods, which dominated the cemetery, were still dormant. Their bare branches didn't help to allay the feeling the place might be haunted. Except for a giant oak with branches that seemed to be waiting to reach out and snatch anyone who got too close, I didn't have a clue what the other trees were. I recognized the oak tree from a history lesson Bonnie had given me about Missouri during the Civil War. I'd asked if she'd been mistaken about Captain Scott having been a Confederate officer because Missouri never seceded from the Union. She told me that most of Southern Missouri wanted the South to win and had no tolerance for Northern sympathizers. It wasn't uncommon to lynch local boys who joined the Union Army from tall oak trees.

Just because there were no cops on the road didn't mean they weren't there. For all I knew, they could be waiting for me on the other side of the cemetery, but it was more likely they were at the scene of the crime and parked in Cramer's drive...if they hadn't already left. The stone building that had protected us from Cramer's gunshot should allow me to spy on the farm without being seen in case they were still there. The only way I'd know for sure was to walk over to the building and peek around the corner. It was the best plan I could come up with on such short notice. Fred had other plans. He jumped out the driver's door and ran toward the cemetery the second I opened the door.

"Get back here, Fred!" I yelled and ran after him.

My shout sounded like I'd used a PA system. The hard walls of the stone outbuilding amplified my voice tenfold. Fred stopped in his tracks and stood with his tail between his legs. So much for stealth. I ran past the stone shack to get him, and froze when I saw an old pickup truck parked by the barn. I grabbed my dog and hid behind a big tree, and not a second too soon. A giant of a man came out the side door of the barn and looked over in our direction. I gauged his size on the way he had to duck coming out of the door. Modern doors are six feet, eight inches. The barn was far from modern, so I doubted if he was that tall, but there was no doubt about his width, he had to turn sideways to get through the door.

After what seemed like hours, but was only a few minutes, the giant turned around and went back into the barn. I didn't know how long I'd have to fetch my flashlight, and I didn't want to chance Fred running away again, so I took him back to the Jeep. This time I only left the window open a crack so even an octopus couldn't get out, and headed back toward the cemetery.

My luck only got worse. The barbed wire fence I'd scooted under the night before had been cut and there were tire tracks leading to the pit I'd fallen in. Evidently, the sheriff had found the body, and probably my flashlight, but I'd never know if I didn't look. At least I didn't have to shimmy under barbed wire. Not only had it been cut, they'd also removed one of the posts holding the wire in place. I was just about to enter the cemetery when I heard the blare of a car horn coming from Bonnie's Jeep. I'm sure I jumped high enough to set a new world's record in the pole vault without a pole. Fred must have stood on the steering wheel in an attempt to escape through the window. The horn stopped almost as soon as it had begun, but not soon enough. The giant came lumbering out of the barn with a shotgun in his hands. I ran back to the Jeep faster than the rabbit at a greyhound track. Within seconds, I had the Jeep started and turned around. Then before I could repeat last night's performance, I saw the old truck in my mirrors race out the farm's driveway and head in the opposite direction.

Fred watched, too, but from the safety of the passenger seat where I didn't need to worry about him honking the horn again. "I suppose if you could talk, you'd take credit for scaring him off, wouldn't you?"

He turned back around and looked at me with a tilt of his head.

I took his big head in my hands and rubbed his forehead with mine before telling him of my new plan. "We got lucky this time, you clumsy oaf. It's time we went to see the sheriff and confess. I'm sure you'll get used to jail food after a while."

I had no trouble finding a parking spot along the curb in front of an abandoned movie theater. Except for more boarded up shops and out of business signs than I remembered from my trip a few years ago, nothing seemed to have changed much in Truman's town square. The sheriff's office was across the street from the courthouse, only twenty yards away. The incident at Cramer's convinced me I'd better tell the sheriff about the body I'd found before he linked me to the crime. My fingerprints were all over my flashlight, and it wouldn't be long before they came looking for me.

The sheriff's office hadn't changed a bit since my last visit. I found myself in a small room with a glass window separating the visitors from the front counter. There was an empty bench along the opposite wall and the remaining wall had a single door I assumed was locked because of the card reader next to it. The white-haired woman behind the glass looked up from a magazine she'd been reading. She put the magazine aside and slid open a small window, but not before I caught a glimpse of the cover. The magazine was one of those "supermarket trash rags," as my mother used to call them. "Can I help you?"

"Yes, ma'am. Uh, I think I need to talk to someone."

She raised her eyebrows and lowered her glasses. "Why don't you tell me your problem, son, so I know who to call?"

"Is something wrong, Connie?"

My back had been turned to the door leading to the offices and jail, and I quickly turned to see a uniformed officer with his hand resting on his holstered gun. He immediately raised his hand when he saw my face. "Speaking of the devil. I was just talking to my deputy about you, Jake."

The officer was none other than Sergeant Bennett whom I helped solve a string of murders the last time I was here. I shook his hand, wondering how fast he could run if I decided to bolt. "Your deputy, Sergeant? Did you get a promotion?"

Bennett smiled and released my hand. I now knew what it would be like to tighten the jaws of a vise on my hand. "You've been out of the loop for awhile, Jake. It's Sheriff Bennett now." His smile was wider than any I'd ever seen on Barney from The Andy Griffith Show. The resemblance was less noticeable than three years ago, but still there. I suppose it was because Bennett had put on a few pounds—quite a few.

I realized my mistake after noticing the stars on his lapel. "Congratulations, Sheriff."

Bennett dropped his smile and narrowed his eyes. "So, Jake, what are you doing in our little, backwater town?"

"Sorry about that," I said, lowering my eyes sheepishly. "I didn't write the blurb in the book. It was my publisher." It was a lie, for I published my own books and had indeed written the blurb describing Truman as a little, backwater town.

Bennett's posture relaxed and the corners of his eyes raised a millimeter. "It's okay, Jake. Except for the reference to Barney Fife, I enjoyed the book. At least you didn't take all the credit for solving those murders. But let's cut to the chase and go back to my office so you can tell us what you were doing at Cramer's last night."

Bennett missed seeing my mouth fall open when he turned to lead the way to his office.

Sitting in a chair facing Bennett's desk was a woman wearing designer jeans and a KC Chiefs' sweatshirt. She either worked out a lot, or had the luck of having an athletic body, but the gray roots in her blond hair hinted at someone who was older than she looked. "Kelly, look who just walked in."

She had already turned toward the door when

we entered but didn't stand. She paused for a second, as if to study me, before answering the sheriff. "Even without the Rockies cap, I'd say it's our main suspect, Jacob Martin."

Bennett laughed. *Did it mean she was joking*? "I'd like for you to meet Deputy Kelly Brown, Jake. They don't come any smarter."

She finally rose, and I held out my hand. She towered over Bennett and nearly met my eyes. I quickly judged her to be about six feet tall. "Thanks for coming in, Jake. I wanted to put out an APB on you, but Chris said you'd show up sooner or later." She glanced over at Bennett when she said it and winked. It made me think there might be a little more going on here than met the eye.

Her grip wasn't as strong as Bennett's, but it wasn't weak either. I wouldn't want to get into an arm wrestling match with her anytime soon. I decided I'd better play dumb until I knew for sure they had my flashlight. "Why would you do that? Did I forget to pay a parking ticket the last time I was here?"

Brown must not have liked my little joke because she shook her head. Her eyes narrowed and I could feel them burrowing into my brain. "Would you like to tell us what you were doing at Cramer's in the middle of the night?"

RICHARD HOUSTON

"Cramer?"

"Come on, Mr. Martin. I don't have time to play games. We have a reliable witness that places you at the scene of the crime."

"Crime? What crime?"

The deputy rolled her eyes and turned toward Bennett. "Can I lock him up now? Maybe a day or two in one of our four-star cells will help him remember."

Bennett smiled and went to sit behind his desk. "Sit down, both of you, please."

Deputy Brown didn't take her eyes off me as we both sat in a couple of hard, wooden chairs facing the sheriff. She finally turned away when Bennett spoke. "I can vouch for Jake, Kelly. He's no murderer. A meddler perhaps, but not a murderer."

I forced a laugh. Obviously, they hadn't discovered my flashlight when they'd loaded the corpse into whatever vehicle had left the tire tracks. I decided I'd keep quiet about it for now with the hope I could still get the flashlight before they did.

"Fred's the real meddler. I just go along for the ride."

Bennett's eyes lit up. "How is Fred by the way?"

"He's great. I would have brought him in but…"
I was interrupted when Deputy Brown's cell went off.
"Brown here, I'm in a meeting. Is it important?"

40

The room went silent as both Bennett and I tried to listen. All I heard was what sounded like a man's voice, saying something about the farm. I doubt if Bennett heard as much as he was several feet further away from the phone.

"Okay, hold on a minute," she said, cutting off the caller, and turned to Bennett. "I'll take this outside, Sir," she said and left the room.

Bennett waited until she shut the door and then continued like the call was routine. "Deputy Brown has been assigned to the Cramer case, Jake. I don't think she'll be as tolerant as I was if she thinks you're interfering with her first murder. She's read your file and might be a little jealous, so please don't try to solve this one."

I barely heard a word the sheriff said. My mind was racing. *Had someone just found my flashlight? Was that what the call was about? It might look a whole lot better if I told them everything I knew before it was too late.*

Deputy Brown came back before I could decide what to do. I was relieved, in a way, I because I knew I'd have said something stupid or incriminating. She took her seat with no mention of why she'd been called away.

The room was awkwardly silent for a moment, and when it was obvious the call was none of my business, Bennett turned his attention to me. "You never did answer Deputy Brown's question, Jake." He was all business again.

"Fred and I were checking names on tombstones," I said, looking at her instead of Bennett.

She looked over at the sheriff before turning toward me. "Fred?"

"My best friend. He's a Golden Retriever."

She tried not to smile, but her eyes gave her away. "Oh. And why were you checking tombstones in the middle of the night?"

I glanced at the clock on the wall and noticed it was almost noon. "It's a long story. Maybe you'd like to hear it over lunch?"

Bennett looked up at the clock the second I said lunch. "Where does the time go? I think that's an excellent idea, Jake."

He stood and reached for his wallet, extracted a couple of tens, and gave them to his deputy. "I'll expect a report on my desk by this evening." He didn't wait for her response and left the room.

She stuffed the money into a small shoulder purse before turning her attention to me. I felt her gray eyes trying to read my mind again. I didn't look away, and it looked like we might end up in a staring match, but her concentration broke when her cell phone went off again. She made no effort to hide the pistol I saw on her belt when she reached for her phone. I hadn't noticed it before because her KC Royals sweat-shirt had hidden it when she was sitting.

She looked at me without blinking an eye. "Do you mind stepping outside while I take this? And don't think about leaving, Mr. Martin. We're not finished despite what Chris thinks."

I did as the deputy told me and waited outside the sheriff's office. The hall was as empty as a Santa Claus convention in July. Even the receptionist who'd been behind the glass window was gone. These people took lunch seriously. I tried looking into the room by holding my hands up against the window to act as blinders, wondering where everyone had gone. There had been four restaurants downtown the last time I'd been here, and I'd only counted two still open on my way in earlier. If memory served correctly, they all had terrible coffee. My mind soon drifted to more urgent matters.

The feeling that something was going on with the sheriff and his deputy resurged when he'd given her cash for lunch. I also asked myself how many deputies can get away with calling their boss by his first name. Those thoughts evaporated when I remembered why I had come here in the first place.

I began to second guess my split decision of not mentioning the body when I realized it hadn't been discovered yet. Then again, maybe I still had time to retrieve my flashlight before they did; or maybe not. Someone had driven a vehicle up to the grave. It must have been so they could load the body, but why hide it from me? Neither Bennett nor Brown hinted at finding the corpse, and the more I thought about it, the tire tracks were far too narrow to be the coroner's van. I squeezed my eyes shut and tried to recall the scene. That's when I realized the tracks were more like tractor or UTV tires.

My daydreaming was interrupted when Deputy Brown came out of Bennett's office. I still had my hands up to the glass window, though my mind had been elsewhere.

"Looking for something?" She caught me before I could look away.

"Just wondering where everyone went. Do they all take off at lunchtime?"

She didn't answer, and stood still, staring with her radar eyes again. Her frown said more than words ever could. "Our lunch will have to wait. We need to take a little ride."

"Can I meet you wherever you're going? Fred's in the car and will need to stretch his legs, among other things."

Her lips opened slightly and her left eyebrow raised showing worry lines around her eyes. "Fred?

Oh, yeah, your mutt. No, bring him with us."

Without another word, I followed her out of the building. Something told me not to try to get ahead of her to hold the door open for her.

Chapter 5

Deputy Brown followed me over to Bonnie's Jeep after we left the sheriff's office. As usual, Fred acted like I'd been gone a year when I let him out. His tail was going faster than a helicopter rotor. "Fred, I'd like you to meet Deputy Brown. She's going to take us for a little ride."

I don't think I've ever seen or heard of anyone changing so quickly. The minute I let Fred out of the Jeep, Deputy Brown seemed to melt. When I asked Fred to shake her hand, he sat on his rear and offered a paw and a smile. "Well aren't you the gentleman?" she said, returning the handshake. She quite attractive, now that I'd seen her smile.

"Mind if I ask where we're going?" It was a question I didn't need to ask because once we'd turned off Highway 65 onto Highway 7, I had a pretty good idea we were headed for Cramer's farm.

Deputy Brown unconsciously scratched Fred

behind the ears. She had one hand on the steering wheel and the other on him.

"Still playing dumb, Jake?" She said it with a smile, thanks to my best friend; albeit it was one most people would call a polite smile, but I took that as progress. Fred was curled up between us on the front seat of her county four by four with his head on her leg.

I tried to give her the best Alfred E. Neuman look I could muster. "What do you mean, Deputy?"

She turned toward me, even though we were on a road with more twists and turns than a roller coaster. "I read your file, Jake, so you can stop the act. If I had your IQ, I wouldn't be working in this cow town." Once more, I felt her trying to get into my head. It was probably my imagination. I'd been watching too many sci-fi movies lately.

"Okay, but what's so important at Cramer's farm that you want Fred and me to go with you?"

"You'll see when we get there." She turned her attention back to driving with an entire split second to save us from going into a ditch. I didn't know if I should be relieved because we didn't die, or disappointed she was no longer looking at me. Her gray eyes were hypnotizing; I felt like I could look into them for hours.

Cramer's farm didn't look as haunted as it had earlier in the morning. The sun had found its way through the morning clouds which made it look more like a scene from an old black-and-white horror movie. If it hadn't been for the half-dozen sheriff's vehicles, it would have been a pleasant picture. Deputy Brown parked on the road by the cemetery in exactly the same spot as I had earlier. She got out of her truck and went over to the coroner's van, but not before telling me to stay put.

Fred sat up on the truck's bench seat and watched the deputy talking to the coroner. The fact that the woman Brown was speaking with was the coroner, came to me from several years of watching CSI. She was dressed in a light-blue jumpsuit and wore gloves like I'd seen the last time I was in the hospital. My powers of deduction were also helped by big yellow letters on the back of her jumpsuit that read, CORONER. She nodded her head a couple times, then pointed toward two guys lifting a body bag into the back of the van. Deputy Brown promptly left the coroner, walked over to the men, and said something to them. Even Alfred E. Neuman would have known the stiff was the same one Fred had found the night before. Ironically, I was focused on Deputy Brown instead of the corpse. Her hair was sticking out the back of her police cap in a ponytail. It reminded me so much of how Julie had looked the first time we'd met. My gaze was broken when one of the men handed her an evidence bag and she turned and headed back toward us.

Fred acted like Deputy Brown was his new best friend when she approached us. His tail wagged and his rear shook back and forth. Brown ignored him and walked up to me. Whatever resemblance to Julie I'd seen was gone, replaced by the frown I'd seen on the deputy's face when we'd first met.

"Is this yours, Mr. Martin?" She was holding the clear, plastic evidence bag an inch from my face. Though I'm farsighted and couldn't focus on the contents, it was impossible not to recognize the Denver Broncos' colors and logo.

"I was going to tell you about that. Honest, I was."

She turned on her mind-reading radar and simply stared.

I began to think about the four-star jail cell she mentioned earlier and wondered if dogs were allowed to visit the inmates. "Okay, it's my flashlight. I lost it when I fell into an open grave and landed on a corpse. I assume it's the one they just loaded into the van."

She continued to stare. Her face was as blank as

a freshly washed blackboard.

"And we were here again this morning," I said.

Her eyes came alive. Someone must have scratched their fingers on her blackboard. "This morning? Before you came to the office?"

"It's why we came in, or rather, I did. I don't think Fred cared one way or the other. When I saw tire tracks leading to the grave, I thought you'd already discovered the body. Then, before I could check on my flashlight, Fred decided to blast the car horn and alert whoever was snooping around in Cramer's barn, so we set a new land speed record and fled."

"Someone was snooping in Cramer's barn? Did you see who it was?"

"No, but he made Jack's beanstalk Giants look like midgets. Oh, and he drove an old pickup I didn't recognize. I didn't tell you because…" I took a deep breath before continuing. "Well, because it made me look guilty. I hope you don't think *I* killed him."

Dimples formed at the corners of her mouth, and I no longer felt her radar. "I know, Jake. Why don't we head back to town? I know a little mom and pop that has the best lunch in town. Then you can tell me what you and Fred were doing snooping around in a cemetery in the middle of the night, and don't give me the lame excuse that you were reading tombstones."

"You know I didn't do it? How?"

Her dimples grew larger. "The coroner said the corpse has been dead for at least a week. You were still in Colorado when he died."

Chapter 6

Deputy Brown wasn't kidding when she said the restaurant was a mom and pop. I expected to see Ma Kettle from the old black and white movies my parents used to watch when I was growing up. What had once been someone's home was now a busy little restaurant. The living room furniture had been removed in favor of a half-dozen, red laminate tables, complete with chrome edges and legs. The chairs were a mismatch of garage sale finds. Deputy Brown didn't waste a Missouri minute getting back to her interrogation once we were given coffee and hand-printed menus from a woman even older than Ma Kettle.

Brown waited for Ma to rattle off her daily specials and leave. "You know you're still a suspect in Cramer's murder, don't you, Jake?"

I'd already decided on the Southern-fried pork tenderloin with mashed potatoes and country gravy, so I lowered my menu and looked into her inquisitive eyes. "You don't think it was suicide?"

She leaned back in her chair, holding her coffee cup with both hands. "Well, it's a possibility. I'm sure there's a plausible explanation on how he managed to wrap bailing wire around his neck, climb fifteen feet to the rafters without a ladder, tie off the wire, and jump. Believe me, it wasn't a pretty sight."

"Bailing wire?"

Brown set her coffee on the table and leaned forward, putting both elbows on the table, resting her chin on her hands. She was absolutely stunning. I wondered if she'd object if I leaned in and kissed her.

"Were you born a pathological liar, or does that come with practice?" She said it with a smile, so I didn't think she'd handcuff me and arrest me on the spot, but I knew I could forget about the kiss.

"Why'd you say that?" I asked, tilting my head to the side.

Her smile disappeared, and her eyes narrowed. "Maybe because you lied to my parents about knowing Cramer, and now you lied to me."

Her parents? I shouldn't be surprised. In addition to knowing everyone in town, it seems they're all related, too. I picked up my menu again to avoid looking her in the eyes.

"Sorry about that. It must be my short-term memory loss."

She leaned in and lowered my menu, forcing me to look at her. "You're incorrigible, Jake." Her smile had returned bigger than before.

"Okay, I confess. I lied about not knowing anything, but I swear I had nothing to do with Cramer's death. The only time I'd seen Cramer was the day before when I politely asked if I could make tracings from some headstones in the cemetery. After he told me—using a few four-letter words—to get off his property, Fred and I came back at night to check it out. We never saw him again until he tried to shoot us for trespassing."

She started to say something but was interrupted by our waitress. I think my eyes must have popped out of my head when I saw my tenderloin—it was huge. Fred was going to have food for a week.

Brown waited for the waitress to leave before picking at her cob salad, and speaking again. "I assume you never had any intention of tracing the epitaphs, so what is it you wanted, Jake?"

I spent the next half hour telling her about how Margot had hired me to look into her husband's great-grandfather's sword, and how I'd found the corpse. It was a story that could have been told in half the time, but I had no intention of letting my lunch get cold. So, between bites of the most tender tenderloin I'd ever eaten, I let her know I suspected the corpse had been robbing graves and had probably been caught by Cramer and shot. I didn't have a clue who killed Cramer, and I didn't care. When I finally finished my story and half my lunch, she drove me back to Bonnie's Jeep with the suggestion I shouldn't leave town for a while.

Bonnie called before I got back to my motel room and I had a chance to call her. I was still on the roller coaster they call Highway 7 and couldn't answer. Highway 7 had to be the deadliest highway in Fremont County, if not the entire state. With drainage ditches on each side of the road deeper than a Florida sinkhole, it would take less than a second to end up overturned, or in a head-on crash with oncoming traffic if one took one's eyes off the road. Once I made it to the intersection of Highway 65, I pulled over and called her back.

"Are you guys okay, Jake? When you didn't answer, I thought they'd locked you up."

"We're fine, Bon. Sorry, I couldn't answer, but the reception is terrible where I was." There was no need to tell her the real reason I didn't answer. She'd lost a daughter on a similar road several years ago. I didn't want to drag up old, painful, memories.

"You said you'd call right back when you hung up on me. You had us worried to death."

"Sorry, Bon, but I hung up because I thought I was about to be arrested. You did say the cops were after me, remember?"

There was a slight pause, long enough for me to hear an echo. I knew without asking that she had her phone in speaker mode and Margot must be listening. "You were arrested?"

"No, Bon, but it scared me enough that I drove over to the sheriff's station."

"Why would you do that? What about Fred? They'd have put him in the pound if they'd arrested you. What on earth were you thinking?"

"I went back to the cemetery to fetch my flashlight before the cops found it, and saw the fence down and tire tracks leading to the grave where I'd found the corpse. I thought it had to be the sheriff. It would look a lot better if I told them I was there before they discovered the flashlight was mine, but it turns out it wasn't the law that left the tracks. The coroner's van is much wider than whatever made them. I'm thinking they might have been there the night before and I didn't see them, which means they were left by whoever killed the stiff. The killer probably murdered him somewhere else and used a UTV or tractor to carry him to the cemetery."

"So, he wasn't shot by Cramer?"

"I don't know, Bon…" I got distracted when I saw a sheriff's truck pull up to the stop sign, and merge onto 65.

"Jake! Are you still there?"

"Ah, yeah. Sorry about that. The signal isn't that great here. I'll call you back when I get to the motel." I didn't wait for an answer. The sheriff's truck had stopped and turned around.

Deputy Brown pulled up alongside me, facing the opposite direction, and opened her window. "Everything okay, Jake?"

"We're fine, officer. Fred had to take a potty break."

She tilted her head slightly so she could see Fred who was sitting up and wagging his tail in recognition. Her eyes seemed to light up. "You really don't have to be so formal. After all, we did have a date of sorts. Why don't you call me Kelly?"

"Sh-sure, officer…ah, I mean, Kelly." I thought I'd cured myself of stuttering when I was nervous, but for some reason known only to my libido, I was doing it again. It must have been her smile.

Her smile turned into a grin. She knew, or at least I thought she knew, she had me hooked. "Well, if you're not having car problems, I guess I'll be on my way. And don't forget to call me if you remember anything you haven't told me about your visit to the graveyard. But this time let's do dinner."

She drove off before I could respond, which was just as well because I'm sure I would have sounded like an idiot.

Chapter 7

The drive back to the motel gave me time to think. *Had Kelly really been serious when she said I was a suspect in Cramer's murder or was she simply trying to impress me?* Either way, I knew I better not say much to Bonnie when I called her back. It would upset Margot that I'd been sidetracked and might have to get involved in solving another murder. I'd gone through several scenarios on how to find Cramer's killer by the time I got back to the motel and called Bonnie. My favorite would not make either of the sisters happy. It looked like Cramer and the stiff had been in the business of grave robbing and were dealing with one or more bad people who killed them both after something went wrong. To find Captain Scott's sword meant I'd also have to find who killed Cramer and his partner.

"Well, I'm glad you finally found time to call us." I knew Bonnie was pretending to be mad in front of her sister, and let it pass. Margot had to be getting on her nerves by now, so I was surprised she hadn't used a few cuss words.

"You know I would have called sooner if the cell phone signals weren't so bad out here, Bon." This little expedition was beginning to turn me into a pathological liar.

"So, are you somewhere you can talk, or are you going to hang up on me again?"

"Yes and no, ma'am. Yes, I'm able to talk now without all of Truman listening, and no, I won't hang up on you again." I answered in the best schoolboy voice I could muster, and spent the next twenty minutes—and the last of my cell phone data—giving her the short version of my meeting with Sheriff Bennett, and Deputy Kelly Brown. I left out the part of how much Kelly looked like Julie. Bonnie had bonded with Julie like a mother bonds with her daughter. I didn't think she'd appreciate another woman in my life at the moment. I was wrong.

"So, tell me about this deputy, Jake. Is she pretty?"

I waited long enough to listen if she had the speaker on before answering. "I suppose. To tell the truth, I really didn't notice."

Someone in the background tried to suppress a laugh. I'd been fooled. She did have the speaker on. "Hello, Margot," I said loudly.

Bonnie continued without missing a beat. "And Bennett didn't have any information on who stole the sword?"

"No, he didn't know there'd been a grave robber until they found the corpse. Neither he nor his deputy seemed to be very interested. I think they're convinced Cramer shot the grave robber, and as far as they're concerned, it's a closed case. They're more interested in finding Cramer's killer."

Margot said something I couldn't quite hear, but I could imagine how she said it. It would have been in a tone both patronizing and condescending. Margot and Bonnie were both twins and widows. Though they were identical twins, an outsider would never know. Margot had married well and never gave a second thought when it came to spending money on her looks, which was one of the things that made her think she was better than her sister. Bonnie had no such luck in the marriage department and had to get by on less than a tenth of what Margot had.

Without expensive spa and salon treatments, plastic surgeons, and ophthalmologists, Bonnie had let her hair go gray, her face sag, and her eyes cloud over. She looked every day of her seventy years, while Margot could easily pass for sixty-nine.

I'd missed Bonnie's reply because I'd been thinking about how I hated the way Margot treated her. "Sorry, Bon, did you say something about Craigslist?"

"Jon found more artifacts on Craigslist." Jon is Margot's son. If he was involved, I knew they had to be worth something. Margot hardly heard from him unless he needed something or he smelled money.

"How's Jon doing, by the way? Is he managing to stay out of jail?" I said it loud enough for Margot could hear.

"Jake! That's not nice. Margot can hear you, you know."

"Sorry, Margot." I wasn't the least bit sorry, but there was no sense in biting the hand that feeds you, and I needed that hand to sign a few checks for me. It's not that that I'm a mean person. The fact is, I would have done almost anything for Margot and her family at one time, simply because she was Bonnie's sister. But Jon has tried to nail me to the wall too many times for me to be nice to him.

"So tell me, Bon, what did Jon find?"

"Jon says someone is selling Captain Scott's knife."

"How does he know they belong to his great-grandfather and not Captain Crunch?"

"Because his name's on it, smartass. Now are you going to find out who's behind this or do I need to hire a real detective?" Margot must not have liked my joke. There was a time I would have told her to stuff it where the sun doesn't shine, but not before exercising a few choice words I'd learned working on a construction crew. It's funny how a mortgage and a dog who eats more than I do can temper those impulses.

"No, Margot. You already have the best sleuth money can buy. Just tell me which Craigslist Jon saw the ad, and I'll check into it."

"What do you mean which Craigslist? Even I know there's only one."

"I've got someone calling in, Margot. Just have Jon email me the ad," I said and hung up. I lied about having another call because there was no sense explaining there were different sites for every major city, and I couldn't stand talking to her any longer.

I doubt if Hell would have frozen over while I waited for Jon to send me the Craigslist ad, but I'm sure the fires would have burned out. I decided not to wait and headed back to Fred's favorite restaurant so I could use the free Wi-Fi to search Craigslist myself.

Fred stood up on his seat, stuck his head out the passenger window, and began wagging his tail at the sight of the golden arches. I parked around back and proceeded to bring up a web browser on my smartphone. When Fred realized I wasn't going inside, he laid down on the seat and stared at me with his sad seal eyes. So much for hijacking Wi-Fi from the parking lot—I had to find a compromise between disappointing Julie and torturing my best friend.

Fred was back to wagging his tail when I got out of the Jeep and looked up to the sky. "I'll order him a plain burger. Will that be okay?" I took it as a yes when she didn't answer and went inside.

The kid who took my order had to consult with his manager before he could ring up a McDouble without pickles, ketchup, onions, or a bun, so I finally settled for a plain burger on a bun. I knew Fred wouldn't mind sharing the bun with the begging jays waiting outside for a handout.

I used the time it would take to fill my special order to search the web for Margot's Craigslist ad. I didn't think the thief would be stupid enough to advertise in the local Craigslist, so I did a global search using the keywords, "Bowie knife and Craigslist." I had a hit in Springfield, but when I clicked on it, it had been deleted by the administrator. They must have spotted the weapon, which is a forbidden item on Craigslist. It looked like I'd have to call Jon and hope he'd answer. Maybe I should have prayed instead of hoped. I left him a message when his voice mail answered for him.

Fred was happy I returned so quickly. He ate his

plain burger in one gulp. The Jays took much longer to eat the bread because they had to fight over it first. I took one more look at the sky to see if Julie approved. It had been cloudy when I went inside the restaurant, but now the sky was clear. I took it as a sign that Julie approved and left before she changed her mind.

We were on a stretch of Highway 7, which was hazardous enough to test Danica Patrick's driving skills, when my phone notified me with the opening bars of Beethoven's Fifth that I had a text message.

I knew enough not answer it. I'd honed my NASCAR driving skills long ago when, as a kid, my sister and I learned to drive bumper cars at the old Elitch's in Denver. She had T-boned my car whenever I wasn't watching, so negotiating a narrow, winding, two-lane road would be certain death if I took my eyes off the road. I waited until we got back to our motel room before reading the text.

It was from Jon, which made me wonder if he'd been prodded by Margot, or was it divine intervention? He'd attached a screenshot of the original Craigslist message. He even had the foresight to expand the contact number. The 417 area code did indeed confirm the poster was from Springfield, so I searched an online directory and found that the number belonged to a Robert Fitzgerald, but I'd have to pay if I wanted his address.

"What do you think, Fred, will Margot reimburse us the ten dollars?" My lazy sidekick had fallen asleep moments after our return to the motel room. He raised his head to look at me with a puzzled look demanding an explanation.

"They want ten dollars before they'll tell me where the creep lives," I answered, even though he hadn't really asked.

Fred rolled his eyes and went back to sleep.

"No more hamburgers for you, you lazy mutt," I said, pulling out my wallet to find a credit card that might not be over its limit to pay for Robert's address.

That finally got his attention. Fred got up, came over to me, and put his big head in my lap, giving me his sad puppy look. I tried to act mad and didn't say anything, but I did reach down and scratched his ears.

Margot's ten dollars bought us a lot more than an address. We also had enough background information on Robert Fitzgerald to realize he wasn't someone to mess with. Robert had spent nearly half his thirty years behind bars. His first arrest was at twelve when he burned down a neighbor's house because she wouldn't return a basketball he'd accidentally knocked into her yard. He was currently on parole and supposedly working as a caretaker's assistant at a cemetery in Springfield. It looked like we had our man. All I had to do now was pass the information on to Deputy Brown, and Fred and I could go home. But first, I needed to bring Margot up to date.

Deputy Brown wasn't in when I called, so I left her a message about Robert Fitzgerald. I finished by suggesting she should consider him her number one suspect and that Fred and I would be leaving for home early the next morning. My call to Margot changed that plan.

"I'm not paying you to find murderers, Jake. If you want to be a cop, you should have joined the police force." Her tone of voice suggested I might have woke her from a nap, or maybe she was having a tooth pulled.

"It's really out of my hands, Margot. I'm sure the sword is long gone by now."

I expected her to exercise her sailor's vocabulary but got silence instead. She was either too mad to talk, or too busy conferring with Bonnie. It didn't take long to find out which. "Jake, this is Bonnie. Margot asked me to talk to you."

"Hi, Bon. How's it going? You ready to check

into the psych ward? I'm sure she's driving you crazy, too."

"Jake! You're on speaker phone."

"Sorry, Margot. Just joking." It was too little too late. I heard her say something to Bonnie that would have made George Carlin blush.

I could tell Bonnie was on the verge of losing it when she came back on the line—Margot had that effect on people. "Jake, I need you to pick me up at the airport. Margot thinks you need some help."

"The airport? That's a three hundred mile round trip."

"It's either me or Jon."

I felt like telling her to tell Margot to send Jon because I was finished, but I already had too much invested and knew I wouldn't see a cent if I lost my cool. "Tell you what, Bon, how about you fly into Springfield tomorrow? I can pick you up after I run by and talk to Fitzgerald."

There was another long pause, while she evidently discussed it with her sister. "Okay, Jake, but please wait until I get there before you talk to him."

"Sure, Bon. Call me back with your flight number when you get it. It's still a ninety-minute drive, so I need to know ASAP. I won't have time to drive down there before you land if you wait until the last minute."

Fred was sitting with his head tilted to the side, looking like the old RCA Victor dog. "Eavesdropping again, Freddie?"

He answered by lifting a paw and laying it on his snout. He made me chuckle and forget my predicament, if only for a moment. It wasn't that I wouldn't be happy to see Bonnie—she'd become a good friend to me and Fred—but I couldn't take her along if I went to confront Fitzgerald. It was simply too dangerous for a seventy-year-old woman. I'd have to finish this business soon, or risk getting her hurt.

Chapter 8

We left Truman before dawn the next morning, taking a back road over to Highway 13 and on to Springfield. I thought I'd be able to sleep in, but Bonnie called back less than an hour after I spoke to her and said she'd be on United's 12:45 flight the next morning. Fitzgerald's home wasn't all that far from the airport, so it gave me plenty of time to swing by his place before picking her up.

He lived in a blue-collar, low-rent neighborhood. The houses were small, probably built in the fifties, but for the most part, well kept. I only saw a few that hadn't seen a coat of paint since Eisenhower was president. The run-down houses had more junk cars in their driveways and front lawns than most used car lots. Fitzgerald's house was one of those. I double-checked his mailbox to verify the address. All the mailboxes on the street were the kind usually seen in rural neighborhoods—bread boxes on a pole. They were designed so the mailman didn't have to get out of his car when he put letters into them. Fitzgerald's was held in place with duct tape.

A young woman in her early twenties answered the door after I realized the doorbell wasn't working and knocked on the screen door. She had a baby in her tattoo-covered arms wrapped in a dirty blanket. I could smell a sweet, pungent odor coming from the room behind her. "If you're the guy who called last week about the sword, you're too late," she said, moving the baby to her hip.

Hoping she didn't notice my surprise or the way I had squeezed my nose muscles, I decided to play along. "You sold it already?"

She must have been too busy with the baby to read my face. "My boyfriend had to hock it last week to pay the rent."

"Did Robert tell you where he hocked it? I could get it and pay you the difference."

She stopped fussing with the child and looked at me closely for the first time. "Are you a cop? Only cops call Bobby, Robert."

"No, just a Civil War collector. Is Bobby in? Maybe I should be talking to him."

She used her free hand to push some blue streaked hair from her face, exposing a nasty bruise near her temple. "The SOB left us last week. Took what he got from the sword and went to that whore in Truman. Didn't even give me no milk money for the kid." Before I could think of how to respond, she turned around, went back into the house, and slammed the door in my face.

I stood with my mouth open, staring at the door. I suppose I could have knocked on the door again, hoping she'd answer and I'd come up with some lame story that might get her to tell me where Bobby hocked the sword, but something told me she didn't know. For all I knew, it was a cover story Bobby had made up to hide how much he got for the sword. I did the next best thing and wrote her a note on one of the business cards I had for my handyman service, asking her to call my cell if she remembered the pawn shop's name. Then I took a twenty from my wallet, wrapped it around my card, and put it through the mail slot in the door. It was probably the first time that slot had been used since the postal service went to using bread boxes on a stick.

Fred started barking at me for no particular reason once I returned to the Jeep. I looked back toward the house but no one was there, and I couldn't see any dogs or cats running loose.

"What's up, Freddie? Do you need to water a tree?"

He answered with a bark I recognized all too

well.

"Okay, let me ask Siri where the nearest park is. Can you wait 'till then? Another bark. I wasn't sure if it was a yes or no, so I didn't waste any more time and found a park less than six blocks away. It was only nine o'clock, and I had several hours to kill before Bonnie's plane arrived, so we drove over to the park.

Fred ran to the nearest tree once I opened his door, but to my surprise, he didn't lift his leg. He sniffed the tree, then went on to the next one. He repeated the ritual a couple more times before he found one he could mark as his own.

I'd been sitting on a park bench watching him when my phone rang. We were the only ones in the park, so I let him explore while I answered it. "Hi, Jake, I got your message."

"You must be psychic, Kelly. I was just going to call you. I think I found the proof I need for you to put Fitzgerald away."

"I thought you agreed not to meddle. Whatever it is, Jake, it can wait. We need to talk. I hope you haven't left town yet."

"Sort of. Fred and I didn't go home. We're in Springfield. I'm down here to pick up a friend at the airport. I did a little investigating and found the guy who posted the sword on Craigslist. It isn't meddling.

73

It's doing what I was paid to do, and track down Captain Scott's sword. But I think I've got the proof that Fitzgerald's the fence behind the grave robberies. He's probably up there looking for another grave as we speak."

"Oh, I doubt that. Not unless he's a zombie grave robber."

I didn't have Facetime turned on, so she must have guessed at my blank look when I didn't respond. "Fitzgerald is the corpse you found, Jake."

Fred had wandered over to the far side of the park where he was sniffing a discarded shoe box. "Fred, get back here, now!" My concern wasn't so much that there was rotten food in the box as much as the Rottweilers in the back of a beat-up pickup that had pulled into the parking lot on that side of the park. A couple of teens dressed like cowboys were about to let the dogs loose. Fred dug his rear feet in and began barking at the Rottweilers.

"Let me call you back, Kelly. Fred's about to get in a fight he can't win." I didn't wait for her answer. Fred wasn't listening to me, so I stuffed the phone in my pocket and ran over to get him. I must have scared off the teens because when they saw me running toward them, they got back into their truck and raced out of the parking lot. Fred looked up at me sheepishly when I got close to him.

"What were you thinking, Freddie?" I said and reached down and took his head in my hands. "Those Rottweilers could have torn you apart." Then I looked into the shoe box.

There was a poor little kitten who couldn't have been more than a few weeks old. The box had been lined with a piece of a worn, wool blanket in an ill-fated attempt to keep the little thing warm. The blanket looked a lot like the one I'd seen wrapped around the Fitzgerald baby. I had no idea how long the kitten had been out here, but by the way it was shivering, it had to have been overnight in near-freezing temperatures. It made me feel like going back to Fitzgerald's and asking his girlfriend for my twenty back. People who'd abandon an animal like this made me sick.

"So, this is why you wouldn't come when I called you?" I said in a much softer tone while ruffling Fred's hair. "You are something else, Freddie." Then I reached down and picked up the little kitten.

Fred barked when I began talking to the animal. "Don't tell me you're jealous now?" I said, putting the kitten back into his box. Fred answered by sitting back on his hind legs and smiling.

I called Kelly back on the way to the airport. Fred sat

in the passenger seat, keeping an eye on the kitten, whose box sat between us. He was acting more like a mother cat than a dog. "Sorry about hanging up on you, Kelly. You were saying something about Fitzgerald being the corpse I found?"

"We identified him yesterday from his prints. He has a record longer than the Missouri River."

She paused a few seconds before continuing in a lower voice. "I probably shouldn't be telling you this, but I'm sure you'll find out eventually. Your guess that he'd been shot by Cramer doesn't hold up for a couple reasons.

"The report from the lab in Jefferson City says none of Cramer's guns have been used lately, and according to Robin, Cramer had no gunpowder residue on his hands."

"Robin?"

"Our coroner, an old friend of Amanda's, and in case you're wondering the other reason Cramer didn't shoot Fitzgerald is that he wasn't shot. Robin ruled out shooting because there are no bullet wounds. We won't know for sure how he died until the M.E. cuts him open."

"So it wasn't Cramer who shot at me then."

"Not unless we're having a zombie invasion."

I felt like asking her if she'd been watching *The Walking Dead*, but let it go. "I wonder what the chances are the same guy killed them both?"

"I'd say pretty good, Jake. Hey, I've got to go, but call me when you get back to Truman. I think you owe me big time, mister, and I know this great Mexican restaurant." She hung up before I could say it'd be my pleasure.

A quick glance at the dash clock told me I still had a couple hours to kill. There was a Quick Stop up ahead, so I pulled in. I grabbed a small can of cat food, and a pint of milk then headed for the counter. The clerk pretended she hadn't noticed me. Her eyes and ears were glued to a TV screen. The same reporter I'd seen interviewing Cramer's daughter was interviewing the mother I'd talked with earlier. The mother had her baby planted firmly on her hip again, but this time she'd switched hips so she could wipe her tears with the baby's blanket.

"I thought he'd left me for his girlfriend in Truman. I had no idea he'd been laying in a ditch all this time. God! What are we gonna do without Bobby?"

The reporter turned toward the camera. "This is Carla Kennedy, live from North Springfield. Back to you, Rick." I wondered if she used a recording for that sign-off. I'm sure those were her exact words last time I'd watched her.

The clerk woke me from my trance. "That's only

a few blocks from here."

I'd been staring at the TV even though they had gone to a commercial. The TV crew must have shown up while Fred and I were at the park.

"Did you know him?" I asked.

The clerk's eyes narrowed, showing crow's feet I hadn't seen before. "Are you a cop?"

"No, not even close, but that's the second time today I've been asked. Do I look like one or something?"

Her crow's feet disappeared when she laughed. "You're too clean cut not to be. You ain't got no tattoos or earrings, and your hair's cut normal. You're either a cop or not from around here."

"Colorado. I'm from a little town outside Denver. You acted like you knew the guy. That's why I asked."

"Yeah, I knew the creep, all right. Ran up a bill and wouldn't pay up for weeks. Then one day he comes in here smiling like one of those happy faces you see on Facebook."

"An emoticon," I said before I realized she hadn't finished.

"Yeah, one of those. Anyways, he not only pays me off but gives me a big tip. I gave it back to his girlfriend the next time I seen her. I knew whatever money they had wouldn't last. He'd spend it on booze or crack. They couldn't afford to blow it, not with that poor baby of hers. She's better off without him."

Fred wasn't waiting at the window for me like he usually does when I got back to the Jeep. He was too busy fussing with the kitten. The cat had managed to get out of its box—with Fred's help I suspect—and was pawing at Fred's snout. Fred had his head on the seat to be at the kitten's level and would flinch every time the feline touched his nose, but he kept coming back for more. I let them play and went around back where I kept Fred's water bowl. I would have laughed if it hadn't been for the kitten's blanket. It reminded me of Fitzgerald's girlfriend and the act she'd put on for the cameras. She hadn't shed a tear while I was there.

Fred and the cat were still at it when I put the bowl down on the floor, picked up the kitten, and set her beside the bowl before pouring a little milk in it. It was the first time I'd had a good look at the cat, but I knew enough anatomy to know I could now refer to it as a she. She went to the milk like she hadn't had a drink in days. Fred watched the scene without taking charge, which was indeed, a first. All of his life, I had put my leftovers down for him, so I expected he would think the milk was his too, but he let the cat lick it clean. I wasn't ready to test him with the cat food and decided to open it later.

Kitty went back to sleep before I found a parking spot at the airport terminal. I knew she would be in good company while I went in to get Bonnie.

Bonnie's flight was early according to the TV screen that displayed arrivals and departures, so I hurried over to where she should exit the secured arrival area. At first, I hadn't recognized her because her hair was no longer gray. The dye job made her look at least a week younger than when I'd seen her last. "Jake, it's so good to see you," she said and came over to hug me.

"You're early, Bon. How was your flight?" I managed to say after she released me from her bear hug, but it had lasted long enough for me to see the gray roots on top of her head that Margot must have missed.

"The pilot said we had a tailwind. I'm glad you got here early. I'm famished."

"They didn't feed you?"

Small dimples formed at the corners of her mouth as she smiled. "Nope. Not even a bag of peanuts. But enough talk about food, it just makes me hungrier. How's my boy, Fred? Is he behaving himself?"

"I'll let you be the judge of that once we get to your Jeep. In the meantime, let's go get your bags."

"What's this, Jake?" Bonnie forgot about her empty stomach and Fred when she saw the kitten. The cat had curled up against Fred in the front seat and fallen asleep, but she woke up when Fred started wagging his tail when he saw Bonnie.

"Fred's new friend. He found her abandoned and freezing in a park not far from here. I'll tell you all about it once we stop to get something to eat."

Bonnie took the passenger seat with Fred and the cat in the middle. "Oh, you poor little thing," she said, picking up the kitten.

Fred stopped wagging his tail and looked up at Bonnie. When she continued to ignore him, he jumped into the back seat and laid down with his head between his paws. I didn't know if he was upset that she ignored him, or the fact she was petting the cat instead of him.

"What are you going to do with him, Jake?" she asked as I pulled out of the airport parking lot.

"I believe it's a she, Bon." I looked into the rearview mirror to check on Fred before continuing. He looked like he'd lost his best friend. "I'd like to keep her, or should I say Fred would like to keep her, but Allison's allergic to cats."

"So? When's the last time she ever came around?"

Allison is my daughter by my first wife, and Bonnie had a point. She has never been to visit me since the divorce eight years ago.

"She's been busy. You know college takes up all her time."

"Well, it's settled then. I'll keep Tigger until you come to your senses."

"Tigger?"

"What else? She looks like a miniature tiger, so I'll name her after Christopher Robin's friend."

I found a coffee shop right before we got on I-44 and pulled in so we could get breakfast before the long trip back to Truman. Once the waitress gave us our drinks and went to put in our order, we returned to discussing the murders.

Bonnie held her coffee cup in both hands and looked at me with her cloudy, gray eyes. "But if Cramer didn't kill the guy who was robbing graves, then who did?" I had just finished bringing her up to date on our morning's adventure, including the call from Deputy Brown.

"Does it matter, Bon? The job Margot paid me to do is over if we can track down the pawn shop where he hocked the sword, and buy it back. Like she said, she isn't paying me to solve another murder."

Mention of her sister made her frown, which in turn made her look every day of her seventy years. "Margot's been complaining constantly about how much this trip has cost, but we're not finished. Are you forgetting about the Bowie knife?"

"No. I've a gut feeling it was hocked along with the sword. Find one and we find it all."

Our search didn't last long. Siri found three pawn shops close to where Fitzgerald lived. The first was only six blocks away from his house. The busy traffic was a complete paradox to the rest of the neighborhood. Most of the stores were empty and boarded up, with only a few liquor stores and second-hand stores left. They all had bars across their windows, including the pawn shop that had gone out of business long before Fitzgerald could have hocked the artifacts.

Our luck didn't get any better with the second pawn shop. It had been converted to a payday loan company. The third shop looked like it wouldn't be long before it became one, too. Except for the clerk, the place was empty.

I was beginning to think a local tattoo shop might be giving out free samples—our clerk's arms and neck were covered in them. She could have passed for Fitzgerald's girlfriend's twin, only she had red streaks in her hair instead of blue. "What's up with Civil War stuff?" she said after I asked about the sword. "You're the second person this week asking if I had one."

"Well, do you?" Bonnie asked. Her tone of voice sounded like she was back in her classroom interrogating a kid who missed a homework assignment. It was the wrong tone to use on this kid.

"I'd ask my boss, but I know he'll say he can't tell you without a court order."

"Would U. S. Grant help?" Bonnie said, sliding a fifty dollar bill across the counter.

The clerk's eyes lit up, and a wicked smile formed on her face as the fifty disappeared into her hip pocket. "It's a start. I'll go turn off the security camera and if Ben Franklin should show up before I get back, I'll get the name and address you want."

Bonnie instinctively looked up at the camera before digging deeper into her purse.

"Let's hope for her sake that her boss doesn't review the tapes," I said after the clerk left.

Bonnie switched her gaze to me. Her cheeks were flushed. "Oh, my. You don't think she'll get fired, do you?"

"Not unless they get robbed after we leave. I'd

think her boss has better things to do than watch security videos."

The girl was back before Bonnie could answer. She had a slip of paper in her hand which she put on the counter but didn't let go. "You're in luck, ma'am. Some guy in Truman bought Fitzgerald's stuff." She inched the slip of paper closer to Bonnie but still held it tightly.

Bonnie laid a hundred dollar bill she had already taken from her wallet on the counter, and the girl let go of the paper and took the money. "If you need anything else, tell Ben he's always welcome here."

I looked at the name and address she'd written and recognized the street name. It was in an area of expensive lake homes. I knew because my sister used to live on the street before she married a local lawyer and moved to DC when he was offered a partnership with a prestigious firm specializing in defending lobbyists. I waited until we were in the Jeep and on the road before telling Bonnie.

"I think this Arnold Benson, or whatever his real name is, lives near where my sister and mother used to live," I said, merging onto I-44 East.

She stopped fussing with her new cat and tilted her head the way some people do when they're thinking. "Where the guy who killed your sister's fourth husband lived?"

"And several other people."

Bonnie went back to petting her kitten when it meowed for attention. "She's lucky you found the real killer. What did the papers call her—the Black Widow?" Fred woke at the sound of what he still considered his cat. I saw him sit up, in the rear-view mirror.

"Yeah, something like that. But luck had nothing to do with it. She wasn't guilty, and the press had no business putting that label on her."

Fred now had his head resting on the front seat, and Bonnie laughed when he licked her on the neck. "I'm sorry, Jake, but three husbands who die mysterious deaths, and all of them leaving her sizeable life insurance policies, does look suspicious."

"Well, that's all water under the bridge. The important thing now is to talk to this collector and see how much he wants for your sword."

Bonnie quit petting her cat because it had fallen asleep on her lap. "Why should Margot have to pay for what's her's? Can't we get the cops to take it from him?"

"Maybe, but I'm sure the lawyers will cost Margot a lot more than he'll sell it for."

"*If* he'll sell it," she said before turning to Fred and scratching his ear.

My mind went back to my date with Kelly, and Fred laid back down on the rear seat after Bonnie stopped paying attention to him. We drove in silence for several minutes while Fred and Tigger slept and Bonnie watched the trees whiz past now that we were out of traffic and headed north on Missouri 13.

The silence didn't last. I was thinking about Kelly when Bonnie brought me back to reality. "Who do you think did it, Jake?"

I could feel her looking at me but didn't take my eyes off the road. I imagined her using her eyes to try and read my mind. I felt my cheeks turn red because of what I'd been daydreaming about. "What? Did what?"

"Kill Fitzgerald and Cramer. What did you think I meant?"

"Oh, well... I don't know. I think Fitzgerald and Cramer were robbing graves and something went wrong. They must have had a partner who killed them both. I don't have a clue who that partner is."

This time I didn't have to imagine her staring at me. A quick glance showed her jaw had dropped and her eyebrows were raised high. "Men—you always miss the obvious when women are concerned."

I turned my head long enough to give her my Alfred E. Neuman look.

"Fitzgerald's wife, Jake. Didn't you say Fitzgerald was sleeping with someone in Truman? I'll bet his wife followed him up there, caught him with his pants down, and then did him in."

It was my turn to laugh. "You're telling me a woman who couldn't weigh more than a hundred twenty pounds kills a man twice her size, then hauls him out to a graveyard, where she tries to bury him? And what about Cramer? How'd she string him from the barn rafters? Oh, and by the way, she's his girlfriend, not his wife."

Bonnie exhaled loudly. "Whatever. Then maybe she had help. Or maybe somebody else did Cramer in. I don't know, but it's obvious she had the best reason to kill Fitzgerald."

"Well, whoever it was, I don't care. Let's get your family relics and go home." I didn't mention I'd been thinking about Kelly and staying on after it was all over.

Chapter 9

Except for a bunch of for sale signs, my sister's old neighborhood hadn't changed much in the five years since I'd been there. It was an upscale neighborhood of professionals and business owners, but Truman's current recession of closed business had taken its toll. Of the homes that weren't for sale, most could use some new paint and a lawn trimming. Arnold Benson's home wasn't one of them. Civil War artifacts must be very profitable. Fred and the cat woke the minute I pulled into the driveway and shut off the engine. Bonnie had been dozing, too.

Benson was standing on his front porch, waiting for us. "Guess I nodded off," Bonnie said, rubbing her eyes so she could see better. "I thought he'd be a lot younger, didn't you?"

"Actually, I'd expected him to be *much* older, judging by the sound of his voice on the phone when we called ahead."

"Everyone around here sounds a lot older than

they are, Jake. I think it's the humidity."

Fred interrupted me with a bark before I could answer Bonnie. "You'll have to hold it, Freddie. Just be a good boy for now and take care of your cat while we talk to him."

"You mean *my* cat," Bonnie said as she opened her door to get out.

Fred didn't seem to care whose cat it was and jumped over the seat and out Bonnie's door before she could shut it.

Benson left his porch steps and came down to greet Fred, who hadn't gone ten feet before sitting on his haunches and smiling. "Aren't you a good boy," Benson said, bending down to pet Fred's head. The effort had been noticeable. It gave me a bad feeling he might not be able to stand back up.

"You must be, Jake. That's one fine dog you have there," Benson said, holding out his hand. He managed to straighten up without help or falling over.

"Yes, I am. Good to meet you," I said, taking his hand and holding it tightly in case he needed support.

"And who's this young lady you brought with you?" he asked.

"This is my neighbor and good friend, Bonnie Jones. It's her family's Civil War relics I called about."

If Bonnie was still drowsy, it certainly didn't

show. Her cheeks were suddenly the color of an overcooked lobster.

"He was my sister's husband's great, great-grandfather," she said softly.

"Well, I seem to be forgetting my manners. Why don't we all go inside? I just put on a fresh pot of coffee, and I'll show you my collection."

Fred barked to let us know he was still there. Benson looked over at him and laughed. "You're welcome, too, big boy. I might even find you a little treat."

Knowing Fred as well as I do, I knew he was more interested in finding a tree, so I let him stay outside instead. It wasn't like I had to worry about traffic. Benson's driveway was a good day's walk to the road we'd come in on, or so it seemed.

The inside of the house was as grand and well-kept as the outside. We entered into a great room through a huge, antique door that had to be ten feet tall. The door was dwarfed by the size of the room with its twenty-five-foot ceiling. Bonnie nodded her head behind our host's back, toward the large Persian carpet covering a marble-tiled floor as we were lead to an oversized, leather sofa.

"What a beautiful view," Bonnie said as she took a seat on the sofa facing some of the largest windows I'd ever seen outside an office building.

"Thank you. We had the home designed around that lake view. It's the main reason I haven't sold, now that Gloria's gone, not that I'd get a fraction of what it's worth in this market." He'd begun his reply with a smile and finished with a frown. One second his eyes were bright and shiny and the next they looked like a cloud had cut off the light. I could feel his pain without having to ask if Gloria had been his wife. I felt the same every time someone mentioned Julie.

Bonnie must have felt the change, too. "Well, it certainly is a beautiful home, Mr. Benson."

The clouds passed and he lit up again. "Thank you, but nowhere as beautiful as you, my dear. And please, call me Arnie."

"How do you manage to keep the place so immaculate, Arnie," I asked while Bonnie tried to overcome her shock.

"That, my boy, is one good thing about the current economy. With our astronomical unemployment rate, help is so easy to find—and cheap, I might add, but it's still difficult to find dependable help. Young people nowadays don't have any clue how to spell work. But enough of my ramblings let me go fetch that coffee." Benson pushed a button on the side of his recliner, and we watched as it slowly raised him to a near standing position.

Bonnie waited until he was out of sight, and hopefully far enough away, so he wouldn't hear. "What an old pervert."

I couldn't help but chuckle. "Now, Bon, maybe you should play along and someday this could all be yours."

She rolled her eyes at me. "Jake! Don't be disgusting."

Benson was back with an ornate serving cart before I could answer her. "I wasn't sure how you take your coffee, so I brought everything I could think of that you might like." The cart carried a silver coffee urn with matching bowls of sugar and cream. There were also several decanters of various colored liquids. Bonnie quickly wiped the smirk from her face she'd given me moments before.

"Is that bourbon?" she asked.

Benson picked up a decanter and held it up to the light from the window. "Yes, it is, my dear. Jim Beam's Distiller's Masterpiece. It used to be Gloria's favorite. We would sit on our bedroom deck on warm spring evenings and watch the boats go by. I've been saving it for someone as lovely as you."

I'm not much of a ladies' man myself, but I knew this was no way to impress Bonnie. On the other hand, I also knew her penchant for bourbon.

She didn't even flinch.

"My favorite, too, Arnie," she said, almost drooling.

Benson smiled, removed the cut-glass stopper from the decanter, poured a few ounces into a thin china cup, and then filled it to the top with coffee. "Bottoms up," he said, handing her the cup.

Not wanting to disturb whatever was going on between the two old coots, I got up and helped myself to coffee. "I hate to interrupt," I said after sitting back down, "but I've got a date with a sheriff's deputy tonight. Could you show us the artifacts, Arnie?"

Suddenly Benson's jovial mood changed as he wiped the palms of his hands down his trousers. There was a sudden chill in the air, as though a wall of ice had formed between us. Maybe I shouldn't have mentioned the sheriff. "I really didn't think you'd show. Most people who call on my ads never do."

Bonnie nearly dropped her bourbon. "Are you saying you no longer have my sword?"

He didn't look up when he answered. "I sold it and the Bowie knife half an hour before you got here." In a way, I felt sorry for the old man. He seemed to age ten years before our eyes, knowing that his flirting with Bonnie was over. I spoke up before Bonnie could exercise her famous vocabulary.

"I'm sorry to hear that, Arnie. Could you tell us who you sold them to? Maybe it's not too late to buy them back."

"I really shouldn't, Jake." He found the courage to look me in the eyes this time, and I could see the guilt he must have felt.

Bonnie's next move surprised me. Instead of showing off her knowledge of words that started with the letter F, she reached over and grasped Benson's knee. "Please, Arnie? It would mean so much to me."

Suddenly, breaking the ice had a new meaning, or in this case, melting the ice. "He's an antique dealer in Lincoln. He called me after he'd found I'd bought the sword. I'll go get his card, but whatever you do, please don't tell him you got his name from me. You two look smart—I'm sure you can come up with a clever cover story."

Benson didn't bother to show us out, nor did he make any more passes at Bonnie. I suppose any chance she had of marrying into money like her sister had evaporated. Fred was waiting at the Jeep, acting like we'd been gone a week. I would have stopped to assure him we hadn't forgotten him but wanted to get away before Bonnie had a change of heart.

"So, when were you going to tell me about her, Jake?"

Bonnie woke me from my trance. I'd been thinking about how lucky my sister had been to have sold her house before the market crashed. But then, she always had been the lucky one—or maybe not, knowing how our mother must be getting on her nerves. Bonnie had been busy with her new cat, and Fred had gone back to sleep on the rear seat, so I'd had a few minutes of silence to think.

"Huh?"

"Your date with a deputy. I know you well enough to know that look in your eyes when you mentioned her. Is she cute?" Bonnie chuckled. I could tell she was having fun with her questioning.

"Yeah. Cute and smart, but I really don't have a date, at least nothing set in stone. I just said that so we could get on with why we went to Benson's before you two sent me packing."

Mention of Benson sidetracked Bonnie's inquiry into my love life, and she went back to petting her kitten.

"Looks like we can scratch him from our suspect list," she said after a few minutes.

"Benson? Since when was he a suspect? And have you forgotten, we're not here to solve another murder. Once we get your relics back, we're leaving Dodge faster than the Clanton Brothers."

Bonnie laughed. I didn't take my eyes off the

road but could imagine the face she must be making. "You mean Tombstone, don't you? Have you forgotten that among other subjects, I taught history, too? The OK Corral was in Tombstone, not Dodge, and only one of the Clantons made it out alive."

"Not my fault, Bon. I missed class the day they discussed the OK Corral. Fred had eaten my homework and I played hooky."

She started to roar and was nearly in tears with laughter. "I'll bet your teachers had their hands full with you." She didn't stop laughing until Fred put his head on the front seat to see what was so funny.

She took one look at Fred and started in again. I'm sure Fred thought she'd lost it, but I knew it was her way of letting off steam. Comedy Central was safe for the moment because nothing I'd said was really that funny. I waited for her stop laughing before I got back to the reason we were there.

"The antique store in Lincoln will probably be closed before we get there. What say we grab a bite then head for the motel? The place is practically empty, so I'm sure we won't have a problem getting you a room."

RICHARD HOUSTON

Chapter 10

"Isn't this exciting, Jake? It's just like old times." Bonnie had been going on about Cramer and Fitzgerald's murders ever since we'd left the motel.

"I'd rather forget most of those times, Bon. Or have you forgotten how close we came to becoming the next victims?" I answered as I pulled into a parking space outside the antique shop. To call it an antique shop was stretching the definition of antique. I could see merchandise through the window that even Goodwill wouldn't take.

"I swear, sometimes you act like an old fuddy-duddy." Bonnie unbuckled and got out of the Jeep, but not before making an exaggerated sigh.

I could feel the corners of my mouth form a smile. She couldn't see it because I was still in the Jeep looking at Fred and his cat. "Hold down the fort, old boy. We shouldn't be long." Technically, Tigger belonged to Bonnie, but the cat didn't seem to know it by the way she was cuddled up next to Fred.

Bonnie already had someone engaged in conversation by the time I caught up with her, so I had no idea if she kept our promise to Benson about not mentioning his name as I had missed the first part of the conversation.

"It's a Confederate officer's sword," she said. The guy she had cornered looked much too young to be interested in antiques. He was wearing a worn out, high school t-shirt. The red and white colors were barely distinguishable, and the Cardinal logo looked more like an Angry Bird caricature than a school mascot. Either the shirt was several years old or had been washed too many times, causing the colors to fade. My powers of deduction put him in his early twenties based on the age of his shirt – assuming he had graduated at eighteen.

He didn't hesitate to answer Bonnie. "I think Dad bought one this morning for that cougar on TV."

I jumped in before Bonnie could betray our trust in Benson, assuming she hadn't already. "He bought it for the TV reporter?"

He hooked his thumbs in his belt and grinned. He started to say more but lowered his head when he was cut off by someone behind us.

"Can I help you?"

Bonnie and I spun around at the same time, as though we were connected like the figures on a cuckoo clock. "Hi, I'm Jake, and this is my friend, Bonnie. I take it you're Kyle Anderson?" I said, extending my hand. "We were wondering if you had any Civil War swords." Whoever coined the phrase about acorns not falling far from the tree must have been thinking of these two. The guy looked like one of those pictures on *Americas Most Wanted* that have been enhanced to show what someone would look like in twenty years. Anderson cocked his head and backed away without accepting my hand. I resisted the impulse to smell my armpits.

"Don't you have something better to do, Jared?" Neither Bonnie nor I went by that name so I guessed he was talking to his son. Jared's shoulders slumped, and he left us without another word.

Anderson turned his fury on us. "How'd you know my name?"

"Jake found it on the Internet when he searched for antique dealers." Bonnie's quick thinking surprised me. Obviously, she hadn't let it slip who'd really given us the tip.

"Jared should have checked with me first. We don't deal in Civil War stuff." He didn't seem as defensive this time but lowered his eyes when he said it.

Bonnie's face tightened. "Are you sure? Your son said you bought a sword this morning."

I could feel the temperature drop. Anderson moved closer, with rage in his eyes. "I told you, we don't deal in that crap. Now, I think you better leave."

"Who do you think he's calling, Jake?" Bonnie asked when we were back in the Jeep. I was in the process of backing out of our parking space but looked up to see Anderson on his cell phone through the store window.

"Let's hope it's not Benson, or your short romance is over."

Bonnie laughed. Not a loud laugh, but the kind Hannibal Lector would make if asked how he liked his steak cooked. "That ended when you asked him who he sold it to. Those two are up to something he didn't want to talk about."

"By 'those two,' I assume you mean Benson and Anderson and not him and his son."

I didn't need to look at her to see her reaction. She hated being corrected. "Of course that's who I meant. Why would I suspect his dimwit son?"

"He could be calling Cramer's daughter."

"Cramer's daughter?" Her tone suggested I'd lost it, so I looked quickly over at her and saw her eyebrows reaching for the sky.

I returned to watching for traffic while I backed into the street. "Your problem, Bon, is you can't think like a twenty-something boy. I'm sure, in his mind, any good-looking woman over thirty is a cougar, and she was the only other female I saw on that broadcast."

"Why would she buy Captain Scott's sword?"

I pulled over to make a U-turn. "Why don't we go ask her?" I said and pulled back onto the highway.

A sheriff's truck was leaving Cramer's as we were pulling in. Sun was shining on its windshield obscuring the driver, but I already knew it was Deputy Brown by the way Fred was shaking the Jeep. It's impossible for a Golden not to move its entire body when wagging its tail. There wasn't room enough for two vehicles to be side by side in the drive, so I pulled onto the grass and stopped. Brown stopped, too, got out of her truck, and came over to our Jeep.

I shut off my engine and rolled down my window. "Morning, Deputy."

Sun reflecting off my window exposed freckles on her face I hadn't seen before. She narrowed her eyes, causing wrinkles to form on her forehead. "What are you doing here, Jake?" she asked, leaning into the open window.

Before I could tell her about Cramer's daughter buying the sword, she saw Fred and the kitten, and her frown turned into a broad smile. "Freddie, are you happy to see me?"

Fred stuck his big head and half his body between me and the open window to get closer to Kelly. She reached over to ruffle his fur. "And you must be Mrs. Jones," she said, looking at Bonnie.

Bonnie suppressed a giggle before answering. "Yes. We're not trespassing or anything, are we?"

"No. Forensics finished up yesterday. I just came by to ask Amanda a few questions and see how she was doing."

"Amanda? You're on a first-name basis with her?" I asked, deciding not to mention what Jared at the antique store had said until I knew more about her relationship with our suspect.

Her smile vanished. "I've known her for years, Jake. So, if you're finished playing detective, do you mind telling me what you two are doing here?"

Bonnie spoke first. "To see if she's willing to sell the place. Me and my sister would like to buy back the family farm."

I turned to Bonnie with my mouth open.

Deputy Brown quit petting Fred and stepped back from the open window. "Why would you want to do that? You'd have to be out of your mind to trade

Colorado for our ticks and humidity."

"Not to mention chiggers," I added.

Bonnie looked at me like I'd just said the F-word and Brown laughed.

"Because this place had been in my brother-in-law's family for generations before his father sold it. My sister thinks it's time she took it back and brought it back to its original glory," Bonnie said.

Brown patted Fred one more time. "You keep your eyes on these two, Fred, I think they're suffering from too much oxygen at our elevation." She looked at Bonnie with a grin wider than the Missouri river. "You're in luck, Mrs. Jones. Amanda's up at the house, and she was asking me if I knew any good realtors. But I should warn you, the house needs a lot of work."

Deputy Brown went back to her truck and left, while Bonnie and I headed for the house. "That was a pretty good story you told Brown, Bon. Maybe you should try your hand at writing fiction. How'd you know not to mention the sword?"

She turned and smiled. "I'm not stupid, Jake. I realized she was a little too friendly with Mrs. Crouch for us to be sharing that information until we know her better, and besides, it isn't a story."

I felt my eyes nearly bulge out of their sockets.

"What? You're not serious? You and Margot want the farm?"

The front door opened and a middle-aged woman came out onto the porch before Bonnie could answer me. The TV broadcast hadn't done her justice. It had made her look a lot heavier.

"You the couple who want to buy the farm?"

Brown hadn't exaggerated about the condition of the house. Two of the columns holding up the roof over the wrap-around porch were rotted out, causing the roof to sag dangerously. I let Fred out of the Jeep while waiting for Bonnie to come around to my side. Tigger had crawled to the far back of the Jeep to take a nap in her blanket, so I let her sleep.

"Don't go too far, Freddie, and whatever you do don't wander over to the cemetery."

He barked and headed straight for it.

Bonnie had gone toward the house in the meantime, so I let Fred go and ran to catch up with her. "Watch your step, Bon," I said as we stepped cautiously over a broken stair tread.

I assumed the woman standing at the top of the stairs waiting for us was Amanda. She was about the same age as Kelly and even had the same hairstyle, but that's where the similarities ended. Amanda was a good six inches shorter and at least that much wider.

"Hi, I'm Amanda, and you two must be Bonnie and Jake," she said when we reached the deck.

It was Bonnie's turn to have frog eyes. "How did you know...Oh, Deputy Brown called you on her cell."

"Yeah, I could take two or three calls by the time someone drives up that driveway. A person better be in shape if they run out of gas on it. It must be at least a mile hike." She had a wry smile that made her plump face rather attractive. It hinted at a mind much deeper than she led us to believe. Sure, it was a long drive, but I doubt if we used more than a gallon or two of gas driving in from the road.

"I suppose you'd like to come in and look at it before we get down to business." She was standing with her hands on her hips and her feet planted like a linebacker, then turned to go inside. "And watch your step on that deck. Got a lot of nails sticking out that could trip you."

I looked at Bonnie and raised my eyebrows. She turned her palms up and grinned before we followed Amanda into the house.

I've worked on a lot of old homes in Denver since giving up my software career, or since it gave up on me. I'd been downsized years ago and didn't have the heart to look for another job, even after the market came back. I've made do with handyman jobs and light remodeling while writing e-books and trying to find an agent for the Great American novel I've been working on since college. I assumed by the age of this house, it would be a lot like the Victorian homes I'd worked on in Denver. It became excruciatingly obvious why the first three letters of 'assume' was a synonym for a mule.

The only thing Victorian about the house was the wrap-around porch. The inside was as plain and boring as a trip through Kansas. There was no fancy wainscoting, coved ceilings, or even crown molding. And forget about a foyer. The plain front door opened into the living room and nearly hit the first step of steep stairs going to the upper level. Amanda was waiting for us just inside the door.

"Well she ain't much, but she's been standing for over a hundred fifty years and will probably be here long after newer homes are gone."

"Or until a tornado blows her away," Bonnie said.

Amanda didn't exactly glare at Bonnie, but she didn't smile either.

"Do you know if the wiring or plumbing has been updated?" I asked. "I don't imagine they had either when it was new, but I can see outlets and a sink back in the kitchen. Bonnie could be looking at a fortune to bring it up to code if they used knob and tube wiring or lead pipes."

Amanda forced a chuckle. "You're funny, Jake. The only code out here is 'Do unto others as you'd have them do unto you.'"

Bonnie's jaw dropped. "You don't have building codes?"

"Nope. Fremont County isn't zoned or regulated. We can pretty much do as we please without anyone telling us how to do it, so I don't have the foggiest idea about the wiring or plumbing. But if you're interested, it has one hundred sixty acres, all fenced, and a huge barn." She stopped talking and lowered her eyes when she mentioned the barn. Neither Bonnie nor I said anything while waiting for her to catch her composure.

"I'm sorry. Sometimes I'd like to burn that barn to the ground. It's where my father died, you know. But, please, let's go into the kitchen. I have a nice bottle of Chardonnay I just opened." Her tone was much softer, almost melancholic, once she was able to speak again.

I grabbed Bonnie's arm to stop her from following Amanda. "Are you serious about buying the farm?" I whispered.

"Yes. I'm sorry I didn't tell sooner," she said, too

loudly.

"Then don't mention the sword to Amanda."

Her eyes grew until they were nearly the size of quarters. "Why not? Isn't that why we're here?"

"Please, just follow my lead. I have an idea." I let her go and hurried to catch up with our host.

Amanda's kitchen was huge. It must have taken up one-fourth the entire first floor of the house. However, like the rest of the house, it hadn't been updated since the sixties. This I knew because of the avocado-green, built-in, double oven with a real clock for a timer. The hood over the range was also avocado-green, but the white range and refrigerator had been replaced within the last decade.

"I suppose it could use a little updating, but she has good bones," Amanda said, twisting the cap off her bottle of Chardonnay and filling our glasses. "They don't build them like this anymore, you know."

I was waiting for Bonnie to say, "Thank God", but she was too preoccupied swirling the wine in her glass, acting like a connoisseur. I took it as a sign for me to get down to the real reason we were there.

"No, and to my knowledge, not many places come with their own cemeteries either."

Amanda's face tightened. "I almost forgot. You

and your dog are the ones who found Bobby, aren't you?"

"Bobby? You knew him?"

"Of course I knew him. I hired him to fix things for us," she said, pushing back away from the table.

"Then you were here when your father died?"

She put her wine down on the table as though it had turned to vinegar. "What is this? I thought you came about the house."

Bonnie jumped in before I had a chance to stuff my foot further into my mouth. "Yes, we did. Jake seems to get sidetracked. Could I ask how much you were thinking of asking?"

Amanda's forearm muscles relaxed and she scooted back to the table, unaware of the scrape she put in the worn-out linoleum. I noticed she didn't reach for her glass. "I really don't know. I was hoping the realtor could tell me that." Her smile reappeared, and she moved closer. "What were you thinking?"

Bonnie hesitated, and I saw my chance to implement my plan. "Would it be okay if we check it out first before she makes an offer? She's willing to pay top-dollar, but wants me to give her an estimate of what I'd charge to make it livable."

It looked like Bonnie was about to cough up her wine.

Amanda's face muscles tightened again, making

her veins bulge. "Livable?" She rose from the table and raised her voice. "This is a farm, mister. Unlike city folk, we don't spend a lot on decorating and the latest gadgets, so if you were expecting an HGTV designed home, you better keep looking."

"Please don't be mad, Amanda," Bonnie said, getting up as well, but not before giving me the evil eye. "He didn't mean it that way. I'm sure he just assumed the rest of the house was like the front porch."

Amanda was standing with her legs apart and arms crossed, the way we'd first seen her, but the veins in her face no longer stood out. Her eyes narrowed as she spoke. "I suppose next you'll tell me he'll want to start in the cemetery. That's what this is all about, isn't it?" Then she turned toward me. "Just what were you looking for the other night when you found Bobby?"

"My sister asked him to check her husband's great, great-grandfather's grave. We thought someone had robbed it and sold his weapons on Craigslist." Bonnie hadn't backed down and looked like she was ready to fight.

Amanda didn't bother answering Bonnie and kept her eyes on me. "So why didn't you ask instead of sneaking around in the middle of the night?"

"I did ask. You father ran me off."

Dimples appeared at the corner of her mouth as she slowly began to smile. She uncrossed her arms and reached for her glass of wine, then sat back down while motioning for us to do the same. "He was a cantankerous old fart, wasn't he?"

After Bonnie and I sat, she offered to refill our glasses. Bonnie beamed, and I waved her off. "You still interested in buying the old homestead, Mrs. Jones?"

"I never lost interest," she answered before downing her wine. "And please, call me Bonnie."

Amanda smiled, making her facial lines deepen. She was far more attractive when she wasn't angry. "You're welcome to inspect the house anytime, Jake. I have to get back to Lees Summit tomorrow, but I'll leave a key under the flower pot on the porch for you. And if our nosy neighbor says anything, tell him to mind his own business."

"Nosy neighbor?" Bonnie asked while passing her empty glass from hand to hand.

Amanda filled hers and Bonnie's glasses again. "Yeah. He used to be the caretaker for the previous owner. He acts like he owns the place, always coming over when no one's home."

"Then why didn't he buy the place when it was for sale," I asked.

Amanda ran a hand through her long hair and

smiled at me. "That's what Pa asked him. You know, Jake, you're a lot like my father. He never had much to say, but when he did, it was always to the point. I like that in a man. Strong and silent." Evidently, the wine had begun to take effect.

"What'd he say?" Bonnie either didn't catch Amanda's change of heart or didn't care.

Amanda raised her left eyebrow in what could have been a wink before turning back to Bonnie. "Said if Pa wanted a border war, he was ready to give it to him."

"Wow, he does sound like a jerk," Bonnie said and emptied her glass.

"That's not the half of it. He and his girlfriend have gone out of their way to be nasty. They even attacked me, for God's sake."

Bonnie gasped and squeezed her eyes shut. "They attacked you?"

"Not physically. She would call me names, like white trash, and flip me off whenever she'd see me."

Amanda paused to drain her glass before continuing. "You know, Bonnie, I wouldn't be surprised if they had something to do with robbing your family's grave. Maybe that's what happened to my Bobby." Her mood turned faster than a jackrabbit being chased by Fred. All of a sudden, her eyes puffed up, and I could see she was on the verge of tears. I knew it was time to leave.

"Well, I better go check on my dog," I said getting up, and motioning with a nod of my head for Bonnie to do the same. Amanda missed it because she had both elbows on the table and was holding her head in her hands.

Two or three glasses of wine had little effect on Bonnie. She also saw we needed to go and got up. "Thank you, Amanda. I'll have Jake come back to inspect the house tomorrow and pass it on to my sister. We should have an offer within the week."

Bonnie waited until we were far enough from the house before speaking. "You could have told me ahead of time why you didn't want me to mention the sword."

I stopped walking and turned toward her, trying to look hurt. "And you could have told me your plans to buy the farm. The idea of having free reign to search for it came to me after you dropped your little bomb."

She lowered her eyes, making me wonder if I'd stepped in something. "Sorry, Jake, but I haven't even told Margot yet," she said and continued toward the Jeep

Fred was waiting at the Jeep for us once we left the

house. He had the biggest smile I'd seen in weeks and a large bone at his feet.

Chapter 11

Bonnie jumped back, covering her body with her arms. "My God, Jake! Is that what I think it is?"

Fred picked up his bone and brought it to her, dropping it at her feet. It didn't look heavy despite it being longer than him. Bonnie's eyes bulged and she backed further away.

I reached down and took Fred's prize, causing her to gasp. "Don't touch it, Jake. It could be evidence."

I threw the bone as far as I could while holding Fred's collar so he wouldn't chase after it. "It's a thigh bone from a deer, Bon. I doubt if the cops would be interested."

She let out a huge sigh and reached for my arm to steady herself. "How do you know that?"

"I don't think I ever met anyone with hooves. Have you?"

Bonnie hadn't spoken a word since we left the farm. I

thought a good lunch might help calm her down and was headed for the catfish restaurant Kelly had taken me to. "Well, Bon, story or not, I think Amanda bought it, hook and sinker."

She turned to answer. Her color seemed to be coming back after the scare from the leg bone. "Let's hope Margot agrees. There's no way on earth I could buy it on my own." She'd been watching Fred and his new best friend after feeding them. I assume she wanted to make sure Fred didn't decide the cat's food looked tastier than his Kibble.

"Have you thought about what you're going to do when you go back to Colorado?" Bonnie asked when I took too long to respond.

"Funny you should ask, Bon. I've been thinking of staying on for a bit. It would be a great place to work on my book."

"Your book? Are you sure it's not because of a certain deputy?"

We were at the restaurant and just in time. That was a question I didn't want to answer. "Hope you like Southern-fried catfish," I said, pulling into a parking space.

The sign above the door read, "Free gas with every meal."

Bonnie took one look at the sign and laughed.

"You can really pick 'em, Jake."

I explained the sign referred to a free sample of their fantastic baked beans. "Well, I hope they taste better than this place looks," she said after we walked in. I'd tried to warn her it didn't have the ambiance of Denver restaurants, but she must not have believed me.

We were greeted by the same waitress as the last time when I was there with Kelly. This time, Ma had her hair in a bun and was wearing an apron out of the forties. I felt like I'd stepped through a wormhole. Bonnie must have noticed because she held a hand to her mouth as we were seated, presumably so she didn't laugh at Ma.

Ma handed us some menus before telling us about the specials. "Our special today is all you can eat catfish. The rest are on the chalkboard behind you, ma'am."

Bonnie recovered enough to find her voice without laughing. "Can I get a Jack Daniels and water before I decide?"

Ma chuckled before answering. "Sorry, ma'am. We don't serve liquor, but the iced tea is really good."

"That sounds great," I said before Bonnie could add her two cents. "Two iced teas it is."

"I'm old enough to order for myself, Jake," Bonnie

said after Ma went to fetch us our drinks.

"Sorry, Bon. Would you like to change it?"

She put her menu down and looked me in the eyes. Any attempt to act hurt was betrayed by the dimples at the corner of her mouth. I knew it was all she could do to suppress a smile. "No, iced tea is fine. And you can order me the special, Mr. Chauvinist."

Bonnie's attitude changed after taking the first bite of the house specialty. "You were right, Jake. I don't usually care for catfish. It's always so muddy, but this is so good."

"And cheap, Bon. I could eat here all week for what a single Denver meal would cost." It made her laugh.

"I swear, sometimes you can pinch a penny so tight it must hurt. I'm surprised you didn't take me to your favorite restaurant, you know, the one with the golden arches."

"Fred's favorite, not mine. Well, it used to be his favorite until Julie made me promise not to take him there anymore." I didn't mention stopping there the day I found about Cramer being murdered.

Bonnie leaned back in her chair and her eyes narrowed. "Were you serious about fixing up the old place if we buy it?"

"That was a cover story, Bon."

She turned her attention toward the wedding

ring she still wore and kept turning it on her finger. "I understand, but if you're going to stay, it might help pay some bills while you work on your book." Her tone of voice made it sound more like a plea than a statement.

"I've been thinking about that. The housing market's so hot in Colorado, I'm thinking I must have enough equity in my place to buy something here for cash and still have enough left over to live on until the book's finished." I'd been avoiding telling her for fear it might upset her.

"That'd be fantastic, Jake." She'd stopped playing with the ring and looked over at me smiling. "I'm sure Margot wouldn't mind if you stayed in the house while you worked on it. And you wouldn't have to do it full-time, so there'd still be time to work on your book."

"Are you sure she wants to spend that kind of money? From what I've seen so far, it's a lot of work. I might have to farm some of it out to subcontractors, and that could get expensive."

"So you'll do it? Oh, I can't wait to tell Margot."

"Whoa, Bon. Don't you have to buy the place first?"

"I'm sure that won't be a problem, considering how loaded she is."

I knew she meant Margot and not Amanda.

"What if you get into a bidding war with the neighbor? Is Margot prepared to pay more than it's worth?"

Bonnie moved closer to the table. "I forgot about him. He sounds dangerous. If he did kill Cramer, he wouldn't hesitate to go after us, would he?"

"I see no reason for him to go after us, as you say."

Bonnie squeezed her lips together and rolled her eyes. "If we buy the house, Jake. Sometimes you can be so dense."

I gave her my biggest grin. "I knew what you meant, Bon. I was just having some fun. But he does sound like the kind who would hang someone with a thin wire and not lose a minute's sleep, so yes, we better watch our backs if Margot agrees to buy the place."

"Oh, she'll buy it all right. You needn't worry about that."

"I'm more worried about what she's going to say about not finding the sword. That was the reason we went there in the first place." Worry over Margot buying the house was the last on my mind. I had bills due, and I needed her to pay me for the time I'd already invested.

Ma returned to ask how we liked the catfish and refill our iced teas before I could ask why she was so sure Margot would buy the farm. By the time Bonnie and the waitress finished discussing recipes for breading catfish and how to cook them, I'd forgotten all about it.

The motel's Wi-Fi was working when we got back to the motel, so I spent the rest of the night in my room, searching for more information on Captain Scott's weapons. I could hear Bonnie arguing with her sister through the thin walls. I didn't find anything more on the relics, but I knew Bonnie must have finally convinced Margot to put up the money because eventually the shouting subsided and all I heard were a few muffled words now and then.

Chapter 12

Fred took off toward the cemetery the minute I opened my door. He'd been sitting between Bonnie and me on the ride over from our motel, and jumped out without warning.

"The key should be under the flower pot, Bon. I better make sure he doesn't get into that deer carcass again." I didn't wait for her to answer and went running after my dog.

"Fred!" I yelled after about twenty yards when I stopped to catch my breath. He was still another hundred yards ahead of me at a section of the fence that was still standing. He stopped for a second before going under the fence, acting like he hadn't heard me. This time I tried a fast walk instead of a sprint. The extra twenty pounds I'd put on these last few years were beginning to show in more ways than one. I made myself a promise to do something about it…when I had the time.

I finally caught up with him at the grave I'd

found the corpse in a few days ago. Fred was sniffing at the edge of the hole like a hound after a rabbit. I thought it odd nobody had bothered to fill in the grave. The first reason that popped into my head was that it was still a crime scene, until I realized there wasn't any loose dirt to fill it with. *How was it possible for Fitzgerald's murderer to dig a hole to bury him without leaving a mound of dirt behind?*

I went over to Fred and knelt down to his level. "Is this where you found your deer?" I expected a bark but got a big smile instead. I had to wonder if Golden Retrievers knew they could get away with almost anything simply by smiling. I took his big head in my hands and laughed. Fred responded with a big wet kiss.

"Ugh. Now I have dog germs on my face," I said laughing while I wiped it off with my forearm. Fred's tail started wagging, and I knew it wasn't because of anything I'd said and turned around.

"You didn't bring a washcloth by any chance, did you, Bon?"

Her eyes were the size of quarters. "Is that Captain Scott's grave?"

"No, it's where I found Fitzgerald. The Captain's grave is over there," I said, pointing to the tombstone I'd discovered just before being shot at the night I'd fallen on top of Fitzgerald.

Bonnie walked over to the Captain's grave and checked the headstone. "I see what you mean about the sword. By the looks of that tree growing in the middle of his plot, someone must have taken his sword years ago."

She walked around the grave, presumably looking for evidence of tampering, before coming back to Fred and me. "It doesn't look to me like he was robbing graves, so why did Cramer shoot him?"

"He didn't. Deputy Brown said Fitzgerald wasn't shot, and Cramer's guns were never fired."

Bonnie raised her voice and bounced from foot to foot. "It's the tractor, Jake. He used it to dig the hole he dumped Fitzgerald in. Cramer must have killed him somewhere else and buried him here."

"That's what I said before if you remember, but now I'm not so sure."

Bonnie frowned, causing the wrinkles on her forehead to deepen. "Why? It's obvious when you think about it."

"The dirt, Bon. Where's the dirt he dug up? My guess is this grave was dug a hundred years ago and never used. Erosion must have washed away the dirt they removed. No, I think my first theory makes more sense. Cramer killed Fitzgerald for trespassing, and the poor guy fell into the open grave. The scene was nearly replayed the night Cramer shot at me."

Bonnie laughed and rolled her eyes. "You just told me his gun hadn't been fired, and who made these tire tracks, smarty? We know it wasn't the sheriff, so who was it? A zombie?"

"Why does it have to be a gun? There are a hundred ways to kill someone without a gun. The coroner said there was no gunpowder residue on Cramer's hands, and the lab report said none of his guns had been fired recently. Most small-county coroners aren't usually trained in forensics, Bon. Most are undertakers or people with little or no training in the field, so I'm not surprised they don't know what killed him. And I never said the tracks weren't the sheriff's. I said they were too narrow to be the coroner's van. Maybe they used a UTV."

"A what?"

"Utility task vehicle. It's like an ATV, but seats only two people and has a bed to haul stuff, like bodies."

She tilted her head slightly as though she was considering what I'd said. "If Cramer didn't use the tractor, and Fitzgerald fell into an old grave after being shot, then... Jake! You don't suppose there's a coffin down there, do you? I mean, if someone dug this as a grave a hundred years ago, wouldn't there be a coffin?"

"It's not deep enough, Bon. I don't think they

finished digging it."

"Or they started to fill it in after burying the corpse and ran out of dirt. That would explain why there aren't any dirt mounds up here, smarty."

I didn't want to argue with her logic and kept it to myself that there'd be dirt left over after filling the hole because of the space used by a coffin, but the idea there just might be a body down there intrigued me. "I'll have to ask Kelly if they found someone besides Fitzgerald next time I see her."

"Kelly? Oh, Deputy Brown. I didn't realize you were on a first name basis already."

I could feel the tips of my ears getting warm. "Or we could always ask Fred to dig up whatever's down there," I answered.

"Jake!" Now her eyes were the size of half-dollars. "Just ask the deputy, okay?"

"Yes, ma'am." I lowered my head pretending I'd been reprimanded like a schoolboy caught with a pack of cigarettes.

Bonnie smiled, wiping away ten years of wrinkles. "You're incorrigible, Jake, and so is your dog."

As if on cue, Fred jumped down into the hole and started digging. We both yelled at him to stop, but not before he uncovered an old blanket.

"That looks like the blanket in Tigger's shoe

box," Bonnie said, reaching down to take it from Fred who had it out of the dirt and clamped firmly in his jaws.

"Drop it, Fred!" He let go of the blanket immediately and lay down with his head between his paws. I'd used a voice he hadn't heard since he was a puppy and pooping in the house.

Bonnie picked up the blanket and patted Fred on the head. "Good boy, Freddie." Her half dollar eyes were back. "I'm sure it's a match, Jake."

"And a hundred others like it. Read the tag."

"Wash in cold water. Made in China." She looked puzzled.

"Exactly. It was made for the mass market, and Wal-Mart probably sold one to every citizen in Fremont County."

"Including our grave robber. What's his name, Robert Fitzsimmons?"

"Fitzgerald. Fitzsimmons is the VA hospital in Denver."

"Whatever," she answered, examining the blanket.

Bonnie held the blanket up by two corners. Her dimpled smile was back. "And I suppose you're going to tell me all the blankets have a piece cut out of them? I'll give you ten to one odds Tigger's blanket fits the cut perfectly."

One look told me she was right. I looked at her then at Fred, who must have known he was no longer in trouble. He'd been sitting on his haunches, waiting for a chance to reclaim his blanket. "Good job, old boy. I'm sure Deputy Brown will give you a nice treat for finding the blanket."

"Deputy Brown? What happened to Kelly?" Bonnie had a grin bigger than Fred's.

I kept Fred's desire to snatch his blanket at bay on our walk back to the farmhouse by letting him retrieve sticks. The trick only worked until he spotted an old International Harvester pickup truck parked next to Bonnie's Jeep. I hadn't seen one of those since I was a kid, and they had quit the pickup business years before that. Fred instantly forgot about the stick and blanket. The big coward tried to hide behind me and started to growl.

Standing by the truck was a giant. I quickly put two and two together and came up with the guy being the one Fred and I had seen the other night when we'd been looking for my flashlight.

The guy had to be six-six and over four hundred pounds. He was huge, but it wasn't his size that was intimidating because the guy had to be twenty years older than me and was more blubber than muscle. It was the double-barreled shotgun he was pointing at us that must have scared Fred. I know it scared me.

"You better have good reason to be snooping around that cemetery. We shoot trespassers around here," he said and pulled back both hammers.

"Whoa, pardner," I answered, stepping in front of Bonnie. "We're not trespassing, and I think you better put that down before it accidentally goes off. We're in negotiations to buy the farm from Amanda and are doing an inspection."

"You know that bitch?" he said, slowing lowering his gun.

Bonnie came out from my shadow when she heard the hammers uncock. "You must be her neighbor. She warned us about you."

He raised his gun and rested it on his right shoulder. But unlike a marching soldier who holds his rifle by the butt, the neighbor kept his fingers close to the triggers. "She tell you her father was a lying, conniving backstabber? The SOB went behind my back and bought the place for twice what's it's worth. It should've been mine. I've been taking care of the place for years and grazing my cattle on the south forty, and he made me move them." His bulging jaw muscles and flaring nostrils made him look like he was about ready to explode. I needed to diffuse the situation before he had a heart attack or decided to use his shotgun.

"Well, I'm not Cramer, and Bonnie's not his daughter, so I'm sure she'd be willing to rent the pasture to you at a fair price if she decides to buy the farm."

"She better if she doesn't want a border war," he answered, relaxing his jaw. "Cramer started one when he kicked me off the land, and you see what happened to him."

He didn't wait for our response and climbed back into his truck. Fred came out from behind me and barked at him when the truck began to back up. Suddenly, the truck stopped and the neighbor rolled down his window. "And you better not let that mutt near my property or he's dead meat."

Bonnie and I were speechless while we watched him back out of the driveway in a cloud of blue smoke. She turned to me, trembling. "Did he just admit to killing Cramer?"

"Sounds like it, Bon, but I promise you, if he touches one hair on Fred's head, he'll see a fate a lot worse than Cramer's."

Fred kept guard on the front porch while Bonnie and I inspected Cramer's house. I think he was still shaking from our incident with the neighbor, or maybe he was just jealous of Tigger. Bonnie's cat had missed all the action by taking a cat nap in the Jeep and was now following her around the house like a lost puppy.

"I think we should report him, don't you, Jake." The remark came out of nowhere. We'd been discussing how I planned to fix the sagging kitchen floor when she said it, but I knew what she meant.

"I'll pass it on to Kelly when I see her," I said, jotting down a note on my clipboard to check out the floor joists in the basement.

Bonnie started to reply when my phone interrupted her. It was Kelly.

"Hi, Deputy. What's up?" I watched Bonnie pretend not to listen by looking around the room.

"Amanda tells me you're about to make an offer. Is that true?"

"Not me. Bonnie's sister."

"How about you tell me all about it over dinner tonight—if you're not too busy, that is?"

I prayed I didn't start stuttering before answering. "Sure, how does six work for you?"

"Perfect. I'll text you the address and meet you there." She hung up before I could agree.

Bonnie grinned when I hung up the phone and put it in my shirt pocket. "You like her, don't you?"

"Didn't your mother tell you it's not nice to eavesdrop?" I said it with the straightest face I could.

"Funny, Jake. You'd know there's no such thing

as privacy if you'd had a twin sister. So where are you going to take her?"

"There's supposed to be a good Mexican place in Truman. Would you mind watching Fred for a couple hours? I can get you something to go."

Bonnie tried to look hurt. "I'm not invited?"

"Bonnie!"

"I was just kidding, Jake. It's been a long time since you've had a date. You go and enjoy yourself. I'll be fine with Fred and Tigger."

Fred's barking interrupted the conversation, so I went to let him in before he started scratching at the front door. "I wouldn't exactly call it a date, Bon," I said, looking out to see if the neighbor had come back before closing the door. I didn't bother to remind her that Kelly and I weren't an item.

I watched Fred go over to Bonnie and Tigger. He ignored the cat and shoved his nose into Bonnie's hand, looking for some attention. His infatuation with the cat must be over.

"Maybe you can ask her why Amanda bought the sword from that guy in Lincoln," she said, scratching Fred on the head. "They do seem to be quite close."

"I can ask her, but I doubt if she knows anymore than we do."

Bonnie sighed heavily. "Well, in the meantime,

don't you think we should search the house?"

I let Bonnie search for the sword while I continued my inspection. There was no use in arguing with her. If Amanda had bought it from the antique dealer, I couldn't imagine why she would hide it in the house and then give us carte blanche to search for it, so I decided to do a top-down inspection and start in the attic.

There was a steep and narrow staircase that went to the attic in one of the second-floor bedrooms. Fred waited for me to climb the stairs and pull the chain on a hanging light fixture before following me. The bare light bulb looked to be from the days of Edison and gave off a dim yellow glow making the attic seem like a scene from the Bates Motel. I let him sniff around some of the junk stored up there while I checked out the rafters and wiring. Unlike most modern homes, this attic's floor joists were covered with one by four lumber, so I couldn't tell if it was insulated or not. I assumed not because there didn't seem to be a huge difference in temperature between the attic and the second-floor bedrooms.

Margot wouldn't be happy with what I'd discovered so far. The wiring was knob and tube and would need to be replaced with modern Romex. I could also see daylight through the cedar shingle roof. It had been nailed to one-by-four, spaced sheeting that allowed light to shine through. I'd heard from some old roofers that it was no cause for concern because the shingles swelled when wet, blocking the rain. Still, the roof would have to be replaced to be safe.

Even more disturbing was the lack of plumbing vent pipes going through the roof. Whoever had installed the plumbing for the kitchen and bathrooms knew nothing about plumbing codes. Depending on when the job was done, the pipes would probably need to be replaced as well if they were either lead or galvanized steel.

I'd seen enough in the attic to keep me busy for a month and decided to check out the bathrooms and kitchen before working my way to the basement where the furnace and water heater should be. "Come on, Fred. Time to go." He was over sniffing out rodents or something by the junk piled in the corner.

He came out from the pile long enough to bark at me before going back in.

"This better be good, mister," I said and went over to see what he had cornered.

His rump was sticking up in the air with his tail wagging back and forth when I made it over to the dimly lit corner of the attic. Edison's bulb barely shone any light on his find, so I pulled out my cell phone and put it in flashlight mode. There were fresh tracks on the dusty floor where someone had recently moved boxes around. I scooted Fred out of the way and removed the box he'd tried to get under.

The box had been covering a loose floorboard. Fred must have smelled a rat or squirrel nest under the floor, so I held him back while lifting a corner of the board. Fred had smelled a rat all right, but this one walked on two feet.

Chapter 13

We found Bonnie in one of the three upstairs bedrooms. She was looking through a cedar chest at the base of the bed and had photo albums, comforters, and bed sheets stacked on the bed. Tigger was sitting on one of the comforters preening her fur, pretending like she wasn't interested. I watched as she checked out a wool blanket Bonnie placed on the bed, then sneak a look in the open chest before turning away. She seemed to smile when she saw Fred, or maybe I'd imagined it because she didn't give him a second look before going back to cleaning her paws.

"Find anything, Bon?"

Bonnie must not have seen or heard us. Her head shot out of the cedar chest and she turned to face me. She looked like she'd been drained by a vampire. "You scared me half to death, Jake. Are you trying to give me a heart attack?"

"Sorry, but I think I can make it up to you," I

said and showed her the sword I'd hid behind my back.

Bonnie's eyes looked like they would pop out of their sockets. "Where did you find it?"

"Better put everything back the way you found it and then let's go back to the kitchen. You can take a shot of that 'medicine' you keep in your purse, and I'll tell you all about it."

It took several shots from her friend Jack Daniels before the color came back to her face. "Margot will be thrilled to get the sword back, Jake, but I don't understand why Amanda wanted us to find it." I had told her how Fred found it hidden under the attic floorboards and my theory that it had been put there for us to find.

"I'm not so sure it was Amanda. Maybe someone is trying to frame her."

Bonnie's eyebrows reached for her wrinkles. "The kid at the antique store! He practically told us where to look."

"Great minds think alike, Bon. Now, all we have to do is solve the riddle of why he wanted us to find it."

"That's easy, silly. Because he wanted to frame Amanda."

"Yes, Bon, but buying the sword isn't illegal, so

what does he have to gain by it being discovered in her house?"

Bonnie's level of excitement dropped a few pegs, and she sat back in her chair, staring at her empty glass. "I don't know. This is giving me a headache. All I know is you did what Margot paid you to do and got the sword back, so please don't go telling your girlfriend about it or she may confiscate it as evidence for whatever crime Amanda was supposed to have committed."

Deputy Brown snuffed out her cigarette when she saw me enter the restaurant. I had been trying to decide if I should tell her about the sword Fred found when I saw the guilty look on her face. I didn't know which surprised me more, the fact she was a smoker, or to walk into a restaurant that allowed smoking.

I decided to honor Bonnie's request and not mention Captain Scott's sword, at least for the time being.

"Hi, Kelly, you sure look great," I said after I sat down opposite her. She was wearing a low-cut dress and had brushed out her ponytail so her hair flowed over her shoulders.

"Thank you, Jake, but all my friends call me Kell." Her expression gave no hint if she was serious or not, and I had no idea how to respond. Luckily, the awkward moment was broken by our waiter.

He set a basket of chips, two small bowls, and a carafe of hot sauce down before asking what we'd like to drink. Kelly ordered first.

"I'll have the large margarita," she said before turning her attention back to me. "It's been a long day, Jake. You have no idea how long."

Our waiter scribbled her drink order on his tablet while asking, "And the Senor?"

"Just coffee, please," I answered. "And I'll have the chile relleno special I saw on your board coming in. Could you make the tacos with soft shells and pollo?"

His face lit up. "Si, senor. And for the lady?"

I looked over at her in time to see her glare at our waiter. "I don't need a man to order for me. I'll take the taco salad."

Our waiter looked confused. I'm not sure he understood every word, but he must have understood her order because he scribbled something on his pad and left. I quickly changed the subject.

"So, Amanda told you Bonnie was about to make an offer on the farm? Were we that obvious?" I did my best to act like nothing had happened and waited for her to finish pouring hot sauce into one of the little bowls. I took a mental note that she passed on the mild sauce our waiter had brought, and went straight for the chile habanero at the end of the table.

She paused mid-pour, holding the hot sauce in mid-air. "She called me to make sure you two were for real. Mandy and I go back a long way."

Kelly just confirmed my earlier suspicion that she knew Amanda a little too well. I leaned in closer to the table. "How far back do you two go?"

"Who's the cop here, Jake? Last I remember, I was the one who's supposed to be asking the questions," she answered, putting down the hot sauce carafe and pushing it toward me.

I grasped at my shirt and tried to squeeze my eyebrows together, pretending to be hurt. "Yes, ma'am. Please don't send me to bed without dinner."

She leaned forward, looking into my eyes. "I wouldn't think of it, Jake. I like my men well-fed before I send them into the bedroom." I wouldn't have been surprised to see her lick her lips. Our waiter broke the awkward moment with our drinks.

Kelly played with the rim of her margarita glass while waiting for the waiter to leave. She ran her right index finger lightly around the rim then brought her finger to her lips and smiled, without taking her eyes off me.

"Did I mention we had a visit from the neighbor," I said, trying to think of something to clear my mind before she had me completely hypnotized.

She dropped her hand instantly. "Which one?" Her gray eyes went dark.

I took my coffee cup in both hands as if trying to extract some warmth from it, and watched her face closely. "I didn't get his name, but I'm sure it's the crazy one. He started by calling Amanda a bitch."

Kelly didn't blink. Either she didn't care, or she agreed.

"Then he points this old shotgun at us and cocks both hammers."

Her eyes actually grew larger. "He did what?"

"Said they shoot trespassers in these parts." I could see her arm and neck muscles tighten, then relax.

"Well, he didn't shoot you or you wouldn't be here, so what happened next?"

I took a sip of my coffee before it could get cold. "I was able to diffuse the situation by saying Bonnie was a prospective buyer, and his attitude instantly changed."

Kelly didn't need to ask me to continue again, I could see it in her eyes.

"So then he tells Bonnie he wants to graze his cattle on the south forty. He said there'd be a border war if she didn't let him."

I paused, trying to remember his exact words. "'Cramer started one when he kicked me off the land,

and you see what happened to him.' His words, not mine."

Kelly stared at me, wide-eyed, and with an open mouth.

I found my mind drifting – wondering how much her parents had paid for such a nice set of teeth. "Yeah, I know. Sounds like a confession. But his next words bothered me more."

"I'm all ears."

Fortunately, she wasn't because I liked her ears just the way they were. "He threatened to shoot Fred if Fred ever trespassed on his land."

Again, Kelly stared without saying anything. Then she shocked me and reached out for my free hand. "Give me a chance to talk to Uncle Mike before you report him, Jake. He hasn't been the same since my aunt died and he took up with that floozy."

"Uncle, Mike?" I answered, pulling my hand away.

She quickly retracted her hand and looked away when our waiter appeared with our food.

I wanted to scream, "Uncle, Mike?" *Why hadn't she said he was her uncle sooner*? Instead, I watched silently as our waiter put our plates in front of us and tried to keep my cool. She busied herself by poking at her taco salad while waiting for the waiter to leave.

She looked up from her study of the different

types of lettuce in a taco salad once he was gone. "Sorry I didn't say something sooner."

"I'm the one who's sorry, Kell. I just called your uncle crazy to your face."

She laughed, causing her eyes to twinkle. "He wasn't always that way. It's only been since he met up with the crazy witch he calls his girlfriend. You should have known him before he bought that stupid farm. We used to come down almost every weekend during the summer when he and my aunt lived on the lake. We'd tube for hours on end then have huge catfish dinners from all the trot lines he'd set."

"Is that when you met Amanda?"

She'd gone back to inspecting her salad but still hadn't taken a bite. "No. I knew her and Robin from Lee's Summit. The three of us went to school together. It wasn't until much later, after my aunt died, that her father bought the farm next to my uncle, and the feud started over the plot he wanted and Amanda's father wouldn't sell."

I watched as she pushed her salad around with her fork. *Was she expecting to see something crawling around in there?* "Wow, I guess it is a small world," I said, wishing she'd take a bite so I could eat my dinner. I was famished, but manners prevented me from eating before she did.

She finally put her fork down and reached for

her margarita. "You have no idea how small a world it is around here, Jake. Stick around and you'll find everyone not only knows everyone else, but they're also related."

"I doubt if I'll be around long enough to meet many of them." I wished I hadn't said it the minute the words left my lips.

"You're not leaving, are you?"

"Oh, I'll be back if Bonnie and her sister ever get the farm. They have this silly idea of hiring me to fix it up for them, but I can't wait while the place goes through probate. That could take a year."

Kelly smiled, still holding her margarita. She didn't seem to be the least upset I was leaving. "If I told you they could close on the place next week, would you stay?"

"How is that possible?"

The sparkle was back in her eyes. "Promise you'll stay and I'll tell you."

"Scout's honor," I said, subconsciously trying to cross my toes.

"The house is in Amanda's name. Has been for a couple years. Her father signed it over after his last stroke, so she can sell anytime she wants."

"Wouldn't her husband have a say in the sale? My sister used to live here, and she constantly threatened her now dead husband because of what she called 'equitable distribution' laws. It's not exactly a community property state, but she was entitled to her fair share."

"How'd you know she's married?"

"I checked out her wedding finger the day we met."

Kelly's eyes lit up. "Oh, checking out my best friend, were you? I think I'm jealous."

I felt my cheeks burning and wanted to bite my tongue, but before I could open my mouth, she turned serious and looked around the room before lowering her voice.

"I shouldn't be telling you this, but her husband was involved in some shady deals and signed away all his rights in return for her keeping quiet. She doesn't need his permission to sell. Your friend can buy the house tomorrow if she wants."

"I'll pass that on to Bonnie. I'm sure she'll be thrilled, but why the cloak and dagger? Even if someone overheard, I don't see why they would care."

She checked out the room one more time, and then went back to running her finger around the margarita glass. "That's insider information, Jake. You didn't hear it from me, okay?"

"Hear what? Did you say something?"

She leaned forward, staring into my eyes

without blinking. "I only told you so you'll stick around. I think I could get to like you, despite what Chris says."

"Chris?"

Kelly leaned back in her chair, smiling. "Bennett, silly. You didn't know his first name?"

"Oh, what did he say about me?"

"Wouldn't you like to know."

"Yes, I would, but if he's anything like his fellow officers in Colorado, he probably considers me a thorn in his side," I said trying to act seriously.

Her penetrating stare was back. "Actually, Chris thinks very highly of you, but I'm not Chris, and this is my case, so don't think for one minute that I'll tolerate your meddling like he does."

I must have hit a nerve. Her body stiffened and she leaned back in her chair. Any thoughts that she might have been romantically attracted to me vanished with the realization I was no more than a stepping stone on her path to solving the murders.

She must have seen my disappointment because she reached out and touched my arm. "I didn't mean that the way it sounded. I really do want you to stick around. It's just that this is my first murder case, and I need to prove myself. I hope it doesn't change anything and you'll stay for a while."

"I'll have to talk it over with Fred, but I'm pretty

sure he won't care one way or another."

"That's fantastic. I can't wait to tell Amanda your friend is serious about buying the house."

I pointed to her salad once she removed her hand from my arm. "Is something wrong with your food, Kell?" I finally asked.

She looked up, a little startled. "Oh, Jake. You're such a gentleman. You've been waiting for me to take the first bite, haven't you?"

Chapter 14

Kelly had been right about the sale of the farm. Within a week Bonnie and Margot had possession of the family homestead. It wasn't a day too soon because the day after Bonnie signed the papers, Margot wanted her back in Denver. Margot was sure her bypass had failed and she needed a nursemaid. I was asked to be the caretaker of the old place and its 160 acres until Bonnie could return. When I asked Fred what he thought about staying on, he became so excited, I thought he might need to see the vet. I didn't think it possible for a dog's bladder to create a puddle the size of a small lake.

Bonnie brought the last of her bags onto the porch for me to load into the Jeep when we saw a late model Lexus come down the driveway. "I wonder who that is?" Bonnie asked.

"Probably neighbors coming to introduce themselves. You better get used to it, Bon. Unlike Denver, people here go out of their way to meet their neighbors."

The driver pulled up inches from Bonnie's Jeep. It was a woman who looked to be in her fifties, with short, bleached hair. She barely came to the top of her Lexus, making her around five three or so. "You the ones who bought the place?" she asked after slamming her door and coming around to the front of Bonnie's Jeep.

Fred thought he'd introduce himself and went up to greet her. "Get that damn hair bag away from me. I paid a fortune for these Marnis."

I rushed over and grabbed Fred's collar. "Sorry, but he doesn't know the difference between Marnis and Goodwill. Come to think of it, neither do I." I didn't bother to introduce myself or offer a handshake.

She rolled her eyes and walked over to Bonnie. "Are you Margot Scott?"

"No, I'm her sister. Can I help you?" Bonnie's voice betrayed her contempt. I knew her well enough to know she had taken a sudden dislike to our visitor.

"Me and my boyfriend own the place next to you. I think you spoke to him a couple weeks ago. We want to know if you're going to give us the forty acres Cramer stole from under us for our cows."

Bonnie's nostrils flared. I expected to see fire shoot out of them. "*Give* it to you?"

The woman crossed her arms and stared back at Bonnie with dark eyes. "We'll pay what it's worth and not a penny more."

Bonnie stiffened and moved to the edge of the porch. "You can tell your boyfriend it's not for sale. Now, I'd appreciate it if you get off my property or I'll have Jake kick you off."

"Okay, lady. You want a border war? You got one," she answered, and got back into her Lexus and raced backward down the driveway.

Bonnie was literally shaking, so I climbed the stairs and grabbed her by the forearms. "Don't let her get to you, Bon. She's evidently not playing with a full deck."

It didn't surprise me when Fred joined us, but I couldn't believe it when Tigger came onto the porch and rubbed up against Bonnie's legs. She reached down and picked up her cat. "Can you believe the nerve of that woman?" she said, hugging Tigger tightly.

"Amanda said she was crazy," I answered and led her back into the kitchen.

She was still shaking slightly, so I took a bottle of her bourbon from the cupboard next to the sink and poured her a glass. She set Tigger on her lap and downed her drink. It disappeared faster than a six-pack at a failed AA meeting.

RICHARD HOUSTON

It was just Fred, Tigger, and me for a few days.
Margot offered to send her son Jonathan out to help
after Bonnie had gone back to Denver, but I quickly
turned down that offer. I told her I'd sooner have a
lobotomy than work with him. She didn't laugh but
agreed not to send him for a while.

I was also told the cemetery was off limits until
Bonnie returned. Ordinarily, that would have been all
I needed to head straight for it. The weather forecast
called for highs in the upper forties with the
possibility of snow on Sunday, so I decided to explore
the 160 acres before it got too cold. Fred was in
heaven when we found a huge pond in the south
forty and decided to try his hand at fishing. Fred's
version of fishing is frowned on in Missouri. It wasn't
exactly noodling because he never once used his
hands—or should I say paws—but then he never
caught anything either. He soon learned there was a
reason catfish have spikes in their dorsal fins.

Our adventures didn't end at the pond. Once
back in the house, I decided to light the wood stove.
Fred's thick coat wasn't much protection from the
cold air after he'd been swimming. We ended up with
a house full of smoke. He finally got to dry off once I
discovered a squirrel's nest in the chimney, cleared it
out, and restarted the fire. Tigger had watched us

shake and shiver from the comfort of a cat bed Bonnie bought her before leaving. Tigger never once offered to help.

Most of the people I knew back in Denver would be having a bad case of cabin fever by now. There was no TV or Internet and the only radio stations I could get were country. After half an hour of switching channels, I found one that reminded me of my father and left it on. The songs were all from the seventies and early eighties. It was the music he loved. Once the house was comfortably warm and both Fred and Tigger had been fed and fallen asleep, I decided it was time to get back to my book. I should have known better. I no sooner booted my laptop than Kelly called.

"How you are guys settling in, Jake?" It was past nine and I found myself wondering if it was too late to ask her over.

"Okay, Kell. We found a huge pond on the farm and Fred tried his hand at fishing today. He didn't catch anything which is just as well or you might have had to arrest him for fishing without a license. Then the chimney backed up and filled the house with smoke, but other than that, not much is going on." I paused while trying to think of how I might ask her to stop by.

"Well, I was wondering if you were bored. It's

karaoke night at the Dam Restaurant and I wondered if you wanted to go."

At first, I thought she'd gone to the same school as Bonnie—I hadn't heard her swear before—then I realized it was "dam" with three letters because of the reservoir in town.

"I'd love it. It gives me a good reason not to write tonight." I hadn't been in a bar since promising Julie I'd quit drinking, but it was a restaurant during the day, so I was sure they'd have coffee.

"Great. I'll see you there in half an hour. Oh, and by the way, it's on the east side of the dam. You can't miss it."

It was raining by the time I made it to the Dam Restaurant. The temperature was also dropping fast which meant the roads would be an ice rink before long. I reminded myself to get back before that happened. Kelly's truck was parked by a couple other pickups, making me wonder if having a sheriff's vehicle in the parking lot was good for business.

The words from Mamas Don't Let Your Babies Grow Up To Be Cowboys blasted from the stage as I entered. Willie didn't need to worry. The guy singing it sounded like Tigger would sound if Fred ever decided to go after her. Kelly was sitting at a table with another woman I didn't recognize. She looked like she was having a great time singing along with the guy on stage, and didn't notice me come in.

I waited by the door for the song to end then went over to Kelly's table during the polite applause. "Hi, Kell. Got room for one more?" I had rehearsed what to say on my drive over but forgot it the moment I saw her. Whatever wrinkles I'd seen earlier vanished under the dim light. Her face seemed to glow. I could tell she was having a good time.

"Jake! I'm glad you made it. I was just telling Robin how good-looking you are and now she can see for herself."

Thank God for the lighting. My ears were burning, and I'm sure my face looked like I'd been in the sun too long. "Hello, Robin. Glad to meet you," I said without stuttering and sat down. Their table was a small round one with a fake candle in the middle. The shape of the table made it so I didn't sit next to either of them nor was there enough light for them to see my embarrassment. Fortunately for me, the next singer started in with a rendition of Coal Miner's Daughter. We all turned our attention toward the stage because she sounded just like Loretta Lynn. It gave me the time I needed to think of what to say so I didn't sound like an idiot.

My thoughts got lost as I listened to the singer and watched Kelly sing along. She was wearing a cowboy hat—or was it a cowgirl hat? Regardless of what it was called, she was stunning, with her long hair down to her shoulders and flowing over her low-cut blouse. The song ended too soon and everyone stood to give the singer a standing ovation. One glance at Kelly made me think of a country classic I'd heard earlier in the day called, *Tight Fittin' Jeans*. Conway Twitty must have had Kelly in mind when he wrote the song.

Robin spoke first after we all sat back down. "Kelly tells me you're a writer, Jake. What kind of books do you write?" Kelly was busy waving down a waitress.

"My bread and butter are how-to-books, but recently I've been dabbling in mysteries."

She scooted her chair closer to the table and leaned toward me. "Really? I love mysteries."

"Watch what you say, Robin, or you'll end up in his next book," Kelly cut in after catching the waitress's eye.

I cocked my head and looked at Kelly the way one does at someone who told a dumb joke.

"Robin's our coroner, Jake."

Robin stifled a chuckle and leaned back in her chair. "Only because the county can't afford a medical examiner. We don't have enough murders to hire anyone full-time."

"Well, in that case, I might have to pick your brain sometime. I could use some advice on the effects of different murder weapons and poisons."

Robin started to reply but was cut off by the next karaoke singer. I would have dropped my drink if I had one—the singer was the woman who had threatened Bonnie with a border war. She was singing an extremely suggestive country song I'd never heard, about a teenage girl and a farmer's son.

"Isn't that your uncle's girlfriend singing *Strawberry Wine*?" Robin asked.

Kelly stared at the singer with her mouth open before nodding her head and facing us. "And she's out looking for someone to sleep with, no doubt. I should call Uncle Al. Grace probably told him she was going to a prayer meeting."

Our waitress finally showed up and just in time. It looked like Kelly was going to lose it. "You guys ready to order?" she asked.

"No," Kelly answered, getting up. "We were just leaving."

The roads were beginning to turn to ice by the time I said my goodbyes to Kelly and Robin and headed toward the farm. I couldn't help but wonder what would have happened if we'd stayed. Kelly sounded like she really hated her uncle's girlfriend, and the last thing she needed as a deputy was to get into a catfight.

Chapter 15

Fred woke me Sunday morning like he does every morning, by scratching at the door to get out. There was at least a half-inch of fresh snow when I opened the door for him. He ran for the stairs, hit the snow, and slid off the porch. Ice from last night's rain had been covered by the fresh snow.

"You okay, old fella?" I asked between laughs. Tigger came to see what all the excitement was about, wearing a huge, Cheshire grin.

Fred couldn't answer, of course, but he let me know in his way that nothing was broken. He got up, shook off the snow, took off running toward a drift over by the barn, and jumped in. A second later, he popped out of the pile and rolled on the ground. I think God must have had Goldens in mind when He created snow. Tigger took one look at Fred and went back into the house.

This was one time I had to agree with Tigger. A thermometer hanging on a porch post said it was thirty-two degrees, so I followed the cats lead and returned to the house, leaving Fred outside to enjoy what was probably the last snow he'd see for a while. I'd no sooner started the coffee when *Beethoven's Fifth* sounded on my cell.

"Hi, Bon. You miss us already?" I said after glancing at the caller ID.

"She's driving me crazy, Jake."

I didn't need to ask who. "Too bad you couldn't take the sword on the plane. Maybe that would have made her happy."

"You think she should be, but no, not a single word of thanks or job well done. You know what she said when I told her about the sword?"

I put the phone on speaker and set it on the counter so I could finish the coffee. "I can guess, but won't use those words in front of women."

"Kelly spent the night?"

"No, Bon. I was referring to you."

"Oh." I couldn't see it, but I could hear the disappointment in her voice. "Anyway, Margot had the nerve to ask if we found the knife, too. Not so much as 'Thank you, Bonnie,' and acted like we'd let her down."

I didn't know what to say, so I said nothing and finished pouring water into the coffee maker before adding the coffee grounds.

"Hello? Are you still there, Jake?"

"Yeah, Bon. It must be a bad signal. You were saying?"

"I called to warn you. She wants to send Jonathan out there."

"Oh?"

"He's been hitting her up for money, so she told him he'd have to work for it."

I counted to ten before answering.

"Jake? Your phone is cutting out again."

I had to keep my cool in case Margot was listening. "Let me guess, by work, you mean take over the repairs on the farm."

"No. You'd still be in charge, but he would help you.

"I've got to go, Jake. Margot's coming downstairs now. I'm sure it's to tell me why she's so much better than me."

I knew I should have got up earlier and gone to church. God must be punishing me for ignoring the Sabbath. It's not that I wouldn't mind having some help, but I knew Jon would be a big pain in the neck. His idea of work was drinking a six pack while telling me I was doing everything wrong.

I was on my second cup of coffee, trying to decide if I should bother with eggs and sausage or simply pop in a couple toaster waffles when Tigger rubbed up against my leg, reminding me I'd forgotten to feed her. Then I remembered Fred was still outside. It wasn't like him to miss a meal.

"Later, Tigger. Let's check on Fred first, okay."

I took her meow as a yes, threw on my jacket, and headed for the door. Fred was sitting on the front porch, watching the fresh snowfall. Tigger ran between my legs toward the barn before I could let Fred in. Evidently, I'd misread her. She didn't want to be fed, she wanted out. It must have been why she'd been trying to get my attention. I'd locked her kitty door last night because I didn't want her out in the cold.

Unlike Freddie, Tigger had no intention of coming when called. She had a mind of her own and treated us like servants. Yelling for her accomplished nothing but a sore throat. I knew she'd probably return when she got hungry, but it was too cold for her to be outside for more than a few minutes. I'd have to get her before she froze or caught feline distemper.

I followed Fred's zigzag path to the old barn after telling him to find Tigger. He used tracking skills passed down from generations of inbreeding. I'm sure a real bloodhound would have gone straight to the barn, but Fred led me to more dead ends than a drunk in a funhouse maze. I knew the location of every rabbit hole and varmint hideout in the county by the time we made it to the barn, but that was soon forgotten when I saw the body lying on the floor.

Chapter 16

Sheriff Bennett exhaled softly, causing his cheeks to deflate. He was trying to console his deputy while explaining what he knew about the body I'd found in the barn. Albert Canfield—or the crazy neighbor, as he had been called by some—was being loaded into the coroner's van after Kelly identified him as her uncle. I'd been asked to wait outside the crime scene tape that had been put up to secure area but was close enough to overhear their conversation.

"Based on the lack of rigor mortis, Robin thinks he was murdered between two and six hours ago, but she's not an M.E., so I'll have to wait for one to come up from Springfield to confirm it, Kell."

"Who could have done such a horrible thing?" Kelly said in a cracking voice. She was trying to keep her composure but was visibly upset after confirming the body was, indeed, her uncle.

Bennett motioned for me to join them. Fred went straight to Kelly. She bent down to pet him and nearly lost it, no longer able to hold back the tears.

The sheriff placed a hand on his deputy's shoulder and looked over at me. "I hope you have an alibi for last night and this morning, Jake."

Kelly stood up, wiped her eyes dry, and spoke before I could answer. "He couldn't have done it last night, sir."

Bennett frowned. "And how do you know that, Deputy?" He was all business again.

Kelly's cheeks became flush. "Uh, because he was with me." She was unable to look her boss in the eyes.

"He was with you? Why would you..." His frown began to turn into a smile. "Oh, I see."

"It's not what you think, if that's what you're thinking. Robin and I met Jake for karaoke night at the Dam Restaurant."

It was time I changed the subject. "Surely, you don't think I'm a suspect. Why would I want to kill him?"

Bennett's smile vanished and he looked straight into my eyes. "Because you're the only one with a motive, means, and opportunity."

"Motive? What motive?"

Bennett took a notebook from his shirt pocket, wet his index finger and thumb then flipped through the pages. "According to a report, his partner, Ms.

Wilson, filed last week, you and Mrs. Jones had quite an argument with him on…" He paused long enough to flip to the next page. "A week ago last Thursday. She says Mrs. Jones threatened to shoot him if he didn't leave, and you told him you'd string him up like Cramer if he set foot on the property again. I'd say that's a pretty good motive."

"That's a lie, Sheriff. I never said any such thing, and neither did Bonnie. He was the one threatening to shoot. In fact, he said, and I quote, 'If she bought the farm and didn't sell him the plot he wanted there would be a border war, like the one with Cramer, and you see what happened to him.' Those were his exact words."

"What about means and opportunity, sir?" Kelly asked. She seemed to have recovered, thanks to Fred. He was sitting at her side, taking it all in. "Anyone could have brought the body here when we were at karaoke."

Bennett smiled politely. "If Al was killed somewhere else, it had to be someone in pretty good shape. Maybe Jake did it this morning."

"If that were the case, sir, wouldn't there have been tracks in the snow when I arrived on the scene? I know Jake's strong, but I doubt if Hercules could have carried my uncle to the barn. He would've had to drag him or drive over in his Jeep."

Bennett looked annoyed. "You're assuming he was murdered somewhere else. He could've killed him in the barn, in which case, there'd be no tracks."

Kelly shook her head. "It didn't start snowing until this morning, so he had to have been killed last night. There was only one set of footprints going in and coming out this morning, and no tire tracks at all. The body had to have been put there last night before it started snowing. Jake was with me then." There was no sign that only a few moments ago she had been crying. There was fire in her eyes.

Bennett raised a hand to rub the stubble on his chin and looked at the snow-covered ground. Any proof of Kelly's statement had been obliterated by the swarm of deputies and their vehicles

"Can the accused say something?" It was time I put in my two cents.

They both looked at me as if I hadn't been there.

"There was a huge puddle of blood under the body when I found him. I'm sure Robin pointed that out."

Bennett cocked his head to the side. "So?"

"If I'd killed him somewhere else, how come there's so much blood? Wouldn't there be blood in the snow if I'd dragged him to the barn? I'm no detective, but it looks like he was killed in the barn. Like Kelly said, my tracks were the only tracks going in or out, so he had to have been murdered last night before it started snowing, and I think I have a pretty good alibi for last night."

He shrugged and started to say something before being interrupted by another deputy. "Sir, I think you'd better look at this."

Bennett looked a little confused, then acknowledged his deputy, but not before speaking to me. "Don't go anywhere, Jake. I need to know exactly what you saw before we arrived."

Fred didn't follow Kelly and returned to my side as we watched Bennett and Kelly follow the other deputy toward the barn. I absentmindedly patted him on the head without taking my eyes off of Bennett. "I suppose that goes for you, too, big boy. Not that we had any of intention of leaving."

Fred barked and pawed me on the leg. "Ouch. Why did you do...?" *Good thing I'm wearing jeans*, I thought before realizing why he had scratched me. A new Cadillac Escalade was coming down the drive.

I'm not sure if Fred wondered what else Amanda was spending her newfound fortune on, but I sure did. I'd heard that those SUVs could go for close to a hundred grand fully loaded.

"What's going on, Jake?" she asked after she stopped next to us and opened her window.

I walked over to her and placed a hand on the jamb. "I'm afraid there's been another murder." I was immediately overcome by the aroma of leather and plastic. There's something about a new car smell that attracts guys like termites to rotten wood.

She blinked a few times before answering, "Oh? Anyone I know?"

"The crazy neighbor, I'm afraid."

"Wow, there is a God after all. It's about time someone gave that creep what he deserved. He made my dad's life an absolute hell. Any idea who did it?"

"I don't, but Bennett was just interrupted by one of his deputies who said they found something important."

She'd been scratching a rash on her arm but stopped suddenly. "Really?" I could see her forearm muscles tighten. "Did he say what?"

"Not a word."

Fred must have lost interest in our conversation when he spotted Tigger on the front porch and decided to join her. Amanda and I both watched as Tigger took off for her kitty door. "I better go get him before he tries to follow the cat and gets stuck in the door again. Why don't you come on inside and I'll put on a pot of coffee?"

"I'll have to take a rain check, Jake. I was in the neighborhood and thought I'd stop by to see how you were settling in." She started her SUV and put it in reverse. "Call me later and let me know what they found, will you?" She closed her window and left me standing with my mouth open before I could answer.

I wasn't alone for long. "Who was that in the fancy SUV?" I'd been watching Amanda leave and hadn't noticed Bennett come back, holding a long knife in his left hand.

"Amanda Crouch, Cramer's daughter." I couldn't take my eyes off the knife.

Bennett shifted the knife to his right hand while raising an eyebrow. "I know who Cramer's daughter is, Jake," he said, while minutely shaking his head.

"But FYI, she's his stepdaughter, not his real daughter—or I should say she *was* his stepdaughter."

Now he had my full attention. "His step-daughter?"

Bennett smiled. "Yep. Married her mother after a nasty divorce. Poor Doris went from one abusive marriage straight into another, but that's not important now. I need to know exactly what you saw in the barn before my deputies arrived."

"The neighbor was lying on the floor, face down in a puddle of blood. I've seen a few murder scenes and watched enough murder mysteries to know not to turn him over, so I wasn't even sure who it was."

Bennett cut me off. "Have a little respect for the

dead, Jake. His name is Albert Canfield."

"Sorry, but as I was saying, I didn't touch anything and left the scene before Fred could contaminate it, and called you."

The muscles in his jaw tightened and he stared into my eyes as he raised the knife. "Have you seen this before?"

"Is that what killed him?"

"Answer the question, Jake."

I squinted my eyes to take a better look. "No, I've never seen it before."

Bennett shook his head and sighed deeply. "Don't lie to me, Jake. Robin said you told her last night that you were hired to find some Confederate relics, including a Bowie knife."

I racked my brain trying to remember if I'd told Robin why I was here. "She must have heard it from Kelly. They both had a lot to drink last night, and she might have been confused. And yes, Bonnie's sister hired me to find the relics, but I never saw the eBay listing of the knife, so I didn't lie to you. Does that mean I'm a suspect?"

He lowered his eyes and relaxed his jaw muscles. "Kelly pretty much eliminated you. I'm asking because I don't have a clue."

"Well, if it helps, today was the first time I've been in there. I've been avoiding it because of the first murder, and if it hadn't been for Bonnie's cat, I wouldn't have gone in today. By the way, is that the Captain's knife?"

Bennett sighed. "The initials, CHS, are engraved on the blade. I assume that's for Captain Howard Scott. Was this knife on eBay with his sword?"

"I'll ask Bonnie the next time I talk to her."

"When will that be?"

"Probably tonight, unless you want me to call her sooner. I could tell her it's a police emergency."

Bennett rolled his eyes. "Call me when you find out, Jake, but tomorrow, okay? I don't need any midnight calls. And see if she can get that picture from her nephew."

The sheriff turned and walked back toward the barn before I could answer or ask about Kelly. I had hoped to invite her in for coffee so I could ask if I really was a suspect. It looked like I'd have to be content with Fred and Tigger, and neither of them were about to tell me what they thought.

Fred and I sat on the porch watching the commotion at the barn. Tigger had more sense and went into the house where she didn't have to freeze. She must have heard about curiosity killing the cat. I wished I had binoculars so I could see the news reporters at the end of the driveway. They couldn't get any closer than the street because it was off-limits to everyone but the police. Bennett must have ordered it taped off after hearing about Amanda's visit.

Eventually, Fred tired of it all and wanted back into the house. It seems the dumb animals were much smarter than the master—they at least had sense enough to get out of the cold. "Okay, Freddie, let's go in and get some hot coffee."

He barked his approval. Or maybe it was his way of saying he'd prefer the cat's milk over coffee.

My coffee pot from the morning was nearly full, so I filled a cup and put it in the microwave. I was in the process of filling Tigger and Fred's bowls with fresh food when someone knocked at the door. Fred forgot about his food and ran to the door. Tigger pretended she wasn't interested in the visitor or her food and walked over to her bed.

"Jake, it's Kelly. Can I come in?" She didn't wait for me to answer and let herself in but didn't get past Fred. He greeted her with his usual wagging tail and shaking torso, so she knelt down on one knee to pet him.

"Hi, Kell. What's up?" I asked after joining them in the front room. "I just put a cup of coffee in the microwave. Would you like one?"

She stopped rubbing Fred's head and stood. Her

eyes were red and her mascara streaked. "Do you have anything stronger?"

I held back on an urge to hug her and reached for a box of tissues Bonnie had left on the coffee table. "Why don't you take these and sit down? I'll fetch you some of Bonnie's bourbon, and you can tell me what's wrong."

Thinking she needed a few minutes to recover, I intentionally took my time pouring her drink before returning. "Try this, Kell," I said, placing the drink on the coffee table before taking the worn-out chair opposite the matching sofa she was sitting in. Amanda had let her father's garage sale finds go with the house. I assumed it was because none of the local thrift stores would take it.

"Thanks, Jake. Why didn't I meet you twenty years ago?"

I answered with the usual finesse I had when it came to the fairer sex. "What happened to get you so upset?"

She took a huge swallow of Bonnie's bourbon and waited a few seconds. "Chris took me off the case and told me to take some time off. I needed this case, Jake. Five years working everything from traffic to meth busts and when I finally get a chance to prove myself, he takes me off the case because someone kills my uncle. It's not fair." She reached for another tissue to wipe her eyes and took another drink from her glass. This time it was only a sip.

"I'm sure it's just policy, Kell. You shouldn't take it personally."

"This isn't Denver, Jake. Policy around here is whatever Bennett says it is." Either the liquor was doing its job, or the thought of being pushed aside had changed her mood one hundred, eighty degrees.

"The jerk thinks I'm too close to the case...and to you."

"Me?"

"Robin must have told him how I was flirting with you last night."

Fred had been sitting by Kelly, listening to every word. I wondered if he understood the complex relationship between men and women—I know I didn't. I wanted to go over and hug her, but couldn't find the courage. A knock at the door ruined the moment.

This time Fred wasn't wagging his tail. He went rigid, and the hairs on his back stood on end. I put the stale coffee I hadn't been able to drink on the coffee table and went to the door.

Sheriff Bennett backed away slightly while rubbing the back of his neck. "Jake, is Kelly here?"

I grabbed Fred by the collar. It was for Bennett's piece of mind. I knew Fred wouldn't bite, but Bennett didn't. "Come in, Sheriff, I was just getting ready to make another pot of coffee."

He wiped snow off his boots on a mat that was too worn to be effective and came in. He looked over at his deputy, swallowed hard, and cleared his throat. "I just went over to break the news to Ms. Summers about her partner's death."

"I'll bet she didn't shed a tear. I'm sorry, sir, but I wouldn't be surprised if she killed him. He probably had enough of her sleeping around and told her to get out. Knowing that bitch, she probably hit him over the head or stabbed him during the argument." The veins in Kelly's neck looked like they were ready to burst.

Bennett stopped rubbing his neck and lowered his eyes. "You're right about not shedding a tear, Kell. Grace is dead, shot in the head. Robin thinks about the same time as Al was killed."

Suddenly, her face turned white and her bulging veins no longer showed. "Shot in the head?"

Bennett walked over and sat sideways next to her on the sofa. "Kelly, I need your gun and badge. I'm going to have to put you on paid leave until we can sort this mess out." I could feel the pain in his voice. He said it the way I had told my daughter I was moving out for a while.

Her bulging vein was back, bigger than before.

"You think *I* shot her?"

"No, of course not, but you know how people talk. And it's no secret how much you hated her. I'll also need the keys to your truck. Robin has volunteered to give you a lift home."

I waited until the last of the sheriff's deputies left before calling Bonnie. I had hoped Kelly would change her mind about going with Robin and ask me for a ride instead. I realized I'd read too much into her feelings for me when that didn't happen.

"Jake, are you psychic? I was just going to call you." It was good to hear her voice after all that had happened, even if she didn't sound happy.

"Hi, Bon. You won't believe the day I've had."

"Tell me about it when you pick me up at the airport. I can't stand another day here."

Chapter 17

Fred and Tigger were both sound asleep in the back seat by the time we made it to I-49 on our way to the airport. The cat fought me when I first tried to put her in the Jeep but was now curled up next to Fred. I would have left her back at the farm after she scratched my arm, drawing blood, but Bonnie had asked me to bring her. I'd forgotten about the scratches by the time we'd driven past Clinton and off the winding Highway 7. My mind had been occupied with the murders and how Kelly was coping. I'd have to give her a call in the morning and see if she needed anything.

Bennett had almost accused her of killing her uncle's girlfriend. More than likely, he'd sent her gun to the crime lab in Jefferson City soon after he'd taken it from her. I assumed the crazy neighbor's death was murder, but now I wondered if it could have been suicide. If Grace was the slut Kelly said she was, it's possible Al killed her, and then himself. But that didn't make sense either. How could he stab himself in the heart and still have time to hide the knife?

Maybe Al caught the killer looking for something in the barn and was stabbed during a fight, but why would the murderer leave the knife at the scene? And if the knife did belong to Captain Scott, how had the killer come by it? Was the killer the grave robber? No, that didn't make sense. I knew for a fact Fitzgerald was the grave robber, and he's dead.

Maybe there would be prints on the knife. It was the least I could hope for. Bennett needed a suspect, and Kelly had to be his prime suspect. She was the only one with means, motive, and opportunity. If the killer was stupid enough to leave fingerprints, it would take the heat off her.

Bonnie called me before I reached the airport to let me know I was late, and I didn't need to park in short-term parking. She instructed me to pick her up at the curb outside the arrivals entrance. I seriously thought about not stopping as I pulled up to where she was standing. I saw a middle-aged man standing next to her, wearing a crumpled sports jacket and a nearly unbuttoned dress shirt. I'd have known her nephew, Jonathan Scott, even without his signature gold necklace. About the only thing he was missing to make him look like the loser he was, was an unkempt, three-day beard. He spoke first when I got out of the Jeep to load her luggage.

"Glad you could finally make it, Jake. What happened? You get lost again?" Jon hadn't lost his charm or the nasty smirk engraved on his face from years of bitterness.

I turned to Bonnie without bothering to answer Jon. "What's he doing here?"

Bonnie shrugged, and let out a sigh. "It's long story. I'll explain later."

"There's no explaining to do. I'm here to finish the job you botched," Jon said. He smiled wickedly and reached into his jacket pocket for a pack of cigarettes, watching my reaction the way a cobra watches its charmer.

I ignored him as he lit up, and turned to Bonnie. "Margot's firing me?"

"No, of course not, Jake. She just thought you needed a little help. Now, would you two get into the car and stop acting like a couple of schoolboys?"

In my younger days, I would have told Jon where his mother could stick her job and walked off. But one thing I have learned from the so-called school of hard knocks is sometimes it's best to settle for crow or you'll end up eating nothing at all. Not that it would hurt me to miss a couple meals, but Fred wouldn't be happy about it. I grabbed Bonnie's bags and put them in the back with Fred.

"So, why don't you bring me up to date, Jake? Do you have any idea who has my great grandfather's sword?" Jon asked between puffs of his second cigarette. He was in the passenger seat next to me. Bonnie was dozing off in the back seat with her cat on her lap. Poor Fred was lying next to her all by himself with the saddest look on his face.

"You haven't heard? We found that days ago. And now I know where his Bowie knife is, too."

"Oh?"

Although I had to keep my eyes on the road now that we were merging onto the highway from the airport traffic circle, I managed to catch a glimpse of Jon's expression. Most clowns would kill to be able to squish their eyebrows together the way he did. It also left the door open for me to get in a little dig.

"Yeah, but unfortunately, the sheriff has it. He's keeping it as evidence in a murder investigation. Which reminds me. The sheriff would like to talk to you tomorrow."

I didn't think it possible for someone to frown so hard that their eyebrows could actually touch. "The sheriff? Why does he want to talk to me?"

"Beats me. Maybe you have some unpaid parking tickets, but more likely, he'll want to search you for traces of marijuana, like he did me. He seems to think everyone from Colorado is a pothead." It was all I could do to keep a straight face when I saw Bonnie awake in the rearview mirror. Her eyes were huge.

Jon flipped his cigarette out his open window. "Oh, my God! I just remembered I forgot to get my bags. I need you to take me back to the airport. Just drop me where you picked me up and I'll get a shuttle to Truman."

Bonnie's eyes grew even larger, and her mouth fell open when I made an illegal U-turn, nearly T-boning a taxi. I didn't bother to tell Jon there were no shuttles to Truman.

"You amaze me, Jake," Bonnie said once we had dropped off her nephew and were back on the road. She was sitting up front with Tigger on her lap and Fred lying between us with his big head on my lap. His woeful eyes replaced by a huge smile while I rubbed his fur.

"Why's that, Bon?"

"Telling poor Jon that Bennett was going to search him. Where did you come up with that?"

I suppressed a chuckle. "Beats me. I only wanted to ruffle his feathers. I didn't think he'd take me seriously."

"Well, I imagine he's halfway to Denver by now. I'm going to have some explaining to do to Margot."

"Tell her that her baby boy needed his diaper changed."

"Jake! That's not nice." She crossed her arms and pretended to pout, but she couldn't keep up the act for long, and soon a big smile crossed her face and she broke out laughing.

I waited for her to regain her composure before changing the subject. "Actually, I lied a little. Bennett had no idea Jon would be on the plane, but he did want me to ask you if you have pictures of your grandfather's Bowie knife."

"Great, great-grandfather, Jake. How old do you think I am?"

"Twenty-three?"

"You need glasses."

"Okay, great, great-grandfather. So, what do I tell Bennett?"

"Tell him I don't have them. I could ask Jon, but I doubt if he'd be willing to help you recover the knife." Her mood had changed faster than a signal light at a speed trap. I couldn't read her face because she was staring out her window, but her voice said her mind was somewhere else.

We drove along in silence for several minutes. Fred and Tigger were both sound asleep, and I thought Bonnie was, too, until she spoke again. "This isn't the way you went last time."

"No, I don't like to drive Highway 7 at night, so I thought we'd take 50 to Sedalia and then go south. It's all four-lane highway that way."

She turned toward me with worry in her eyes. "We do need to get the knife back pretty soon, or Margot's going to send Jonathan back."

"I have a feeling she'll send him regardless, or are you forgetting all the repairs needed on the farm? The fact that I'm twice the carpenter he'll ever be doesn't matter when it comes to family."

She turned back toward the window again. "No, I haven't forgotten, and neither has Margot."

I let Bonnie sleep in the next morning while Fred and I walked around the farm. She had taken over Cramer's old bedroom on the upper floor, and Fred and I had settled into the sunroom on the lower level. The old house had three bedrooms and a bathroom upstairs, but only Cramer's was livable because of the leaking roof. The sunroom, on the other hand, had been added on sometime in the last decade, so all I had to do to make it a temporary bedroom was tack some sheets onto the French doors leading to the living room, and move in a used bed I'd picked up at one of Truman's many junk stores. There was also a bathroom—slash laundry room—I was able to use without waking Bonnie. The bathroom looked like it had been added on about the same time as the sunroom. How the original occupants managed to raise a dozen kids with only three bedrooms and a single upstairs bath I'd never know.

I also called Kelly twice and each time got her voice mail. Both times I left a message asking how she was doing and if she needed anything. I wanted to ask if she needed a hug but thought she might take it the wrong way. What she really needed was for someone to find out who killed her uncle and his girlfriend.

Some innate feeling told me all the murders were connected to Captain Scott's weapons, so I had the brilliant idea to start at the beginning and revisit the cemetery. Fred must have had the same idea because he was a hundred yards ahead of me sniffing the hallowed ground. I'd expected him to head for Captain Scott's grave, but he was hot on some critter's trail and heading in the opposite direction.

"Whoa, Fred! Wait up," I yelled, running to catch up with him. I might as well have been yelling at the trees. Fred ducked under the rickety fence surrounding the headstones and went straight toward the caretaker's shed. I needed to pick up the pace before he disturbed a den of skunks or copperheads.

He was nowhere in sight by the time I got to the shed, so I cautiously pushed aside some of the vines that were growing everywhere and stepped inside through a doorless entry. The shed had been constructed from fieldstone and would probably stand another 150 years, but the door and window frames had long ago rotted away. I was surprised to see the rest of the shack intact until I noticed it was protected from the weather by a newer metal roof. Along a windowless wall stood a homemade tool cabinet with open doors. The only tools in it were a pick and shovel with bright-yellow, fiberglass handles, which I knew without searching the Internet didn't exist 150 years ago. Someone must have been here recently. I found Fred sniffing at the base of the cabinet.

"What've you got there, boy?" I asked after kneeling down to his level and saw that the cabinet had been hiding something more sinister. There were tracks on the dusty floor indicating the cabinet had been moved recently. I lied down to examine the bottom of the cabinet, and Fred started licking my face. He must have thought I wanted to play.

I quickly sat up to wipe off my face, and inadvertently pushed against the cabinet, causing it to move. It had been covering a hidden stairway.

Fred forgot about cleaning my face and raced

down the stairs before I had a chance to stop him. "Get back here, Fred!" I yelled, too late. What little light that shone through an east-facing window gave no hint he was down there. I had no choice but to follow him.

The room below the caretaker's shack had floor to ceiling shelves along each wall, stocked with old Mason jars. I couldn't see what was in them in the dim light, but I realized it must have been a root cellar, built before modern refrigeration. It wasn't until I fished out my smartphone and turned on its flashlight that I saw half the room was filled with freshly dug dirt from a tunnel. Fred had disappeared into the tunnel. It was too big to have been dug by a groundhog or whatever Fred had been chasing, and it didn't take a Mensa candidate to put two and two together and come up with how Fitzgerald had robbed the graveyard without disturbing the surface. It also didn't take much imagination to recognize it must have been a tunnel collapse that killed Fitzgerald, and if I didn't get Fred out of there soon, it could happen to him.

"Fred, come here boy." I didn't want to yell for fear I might cause another collapse, so I said it softly. When he didn't show, I decided to crawl into the hole a few feet and shine my light. I've done a lot of stupid things in my life, and I was about to add one more to the list by going after him when I saw two reflective dots coming slowly toward me, and I silently said a little prayer that the ground didn't cave in before he came to me.

"Good boy, Freddie. Keep coming. That's a boy. I promise I'm not mad at you," I said and backed out of the tunnel. When he got close enough, I grabbed his collar and dragged him the rest of the way out. Although I had lied about not being mad, I soon forgot and gave him a big bear hug. I was so relieved to have him back that I didn't notice the piece of blanket he had in his mouth.

Chapter 18

Bonnie held the scrap of blanket up to the light streaming in through the kitchen window. Then she held Tigger's blanket next to it. "It's the same pattern, Jake. They both feel like some kind of cheap synthetic, but the colors don't match."

"I wonder if it matches the blanket Fred found at Fitzgerald's grave?"

Bonnie smiled before answering. "Too bad you gave that blanket to your girlfriend, but I'm sure she wouldn't mind checking it out for you."

"Kelly's not my girlfriend, Bon."

Bonnie rolled her eyes and twisted her smile into a frown. "Yeah, and I'm Mother Teresa. We don't need her anyway," she said, holding the blankets back up to the light. "Neither of these are old enough to have come from a coffin in that cemetery, so that means someone probably bought them from a store recently."

"And chances are that someone is none other

than Fitzgerald's wife. Remember I told you her baby was wrapped in a similar blanket just before I picked you up at the airport the first time?"

Bonnie's eyes lit up. "So that proves her husband was the grave robber."

"Maybe in our eyes. I'm sure a smart lawyer will call it circumstantial evidence, but we already knew Fitzgerald was the grave robber. What we didn't know is that he died in a cave-in, and not murdered like everyone thinks."

"So he wasn't killed for the Captain's sword?"

"Not by a long shot. I believe he was using those cheap blankets to line the tunnel, a tunnel that more than likely runs to Captain Scott's grave. That explains how he came by the sword he hocked. He really did rob the Captain's grave, and probably a whole bunch more."

Bonnie put the blankets down on the kitchen table and sat down on the chair closest to them. "Then who killed Cramer and the neighbor?"

"Who had a motive?"

She stared at me blankly, so I asked another question. "Can you think of something Cramer and the neighbors had that someone might want to kill for?"

There was complete silence while I imagined the wheels in her head turning. "Only the land the crazy neighbor wanted, but if he killed Cramer, who killed him and his girlfriend?" she answered.

"Actually, the question was rhetorical. Al might have killed Cramer over it, but who had a motive to kill him and his girlfriend?"

Bonnie tilted her head slightly as if the answer was stuck up there and she could shake it out. "I don't know, Jake."

"Me either, and I'm afraid Kelly is the number one suspect at the moment. She made her hatred of Grace very clear Saturday night—at least, that's what the sheriff must think. He suspended her and took away her gun and badge."

Bonnie's shoulders tightened and the color seemed to drain from her face. "Maybe it's the sword and knife? I could be next if the murderer finds out I have the sword."

I went over to the table and put my hand on her shoulder. "Not as long as Fred and I are still breathing. Right, Freddie?"

Fred had been dozing but raised his head at the mention of his name. I looked him in the eyes and asked again. This time we got a bark that brought a smile back to Bonnie's face.

Yesterday's snow had melted and the forecast was for a high near sixty. One thing Missouri had in common with Colorado was the adage, "If you don't like the weather, wait fifteen minutes, and it will change." It seemed to be a cliché all weathermen used to explain their mistaken predictions. I wasn't complaining, and neither was Fred as we went outside to call Kelly back. Well, maybe that's not why Fred joined me, but I'm sure he was a little curious as to why she hadn't returned any of my calls.

Kelly answered on the second ring. "Sorry I didn't call you back, Jake, but Chris has been here all morning, and I didn't have a chance." She sounded like she'd been crying.

"Is something wrong, Kell?"

There was a long pause. "Oh, Jake. They think I killed my uncle and his girlfriend. Why would I want him dead? I loved him."

"Someone was with Bennett?"

"Robin. I thought she was my friend." This time I detected anger in her voice. "Can you come over, Jake? I need your help."

"How about we meet somewhere? It's not that I'm paranoid, but *they* may be watching, and your boss has already told me not to meddle." I'd said the word 'they' like it was something that tasted terrible.

Kelly had chosen a bar I knew well. It was the same one I used to frequent last time I'd been here to help my sister when she'd been accused of murder. I felt like the character in Groundhog Day who lived the same day over and over until he got it right.

"Hi, Kell," I said, taking a chair at the table she'd chosen before I got there—it was a table I knew all too well.

The table was set along the wall next to large windows with a view of the lake. She looked so innocent with the sun shining on her golden hair. One would never imagine she was a murder suspect. "Thanks, Jake. I'm so glad you came. I don't know who I can trust anymore."

"Tell me everything, Kell. I don't know how I can help you, but I will if I can."

"It's a long story—I'll need another drink first." She reached for an empty glass and waved at the bartender. I'd already noticed the change in personnel, so I didn't worry about getting caught up in a conversation about old times with the hired help.

Once Kelly ordered her wine and I ordered my coffee, she began. "They questioned me like some kind of criminal. I couldn't believe it."

"By 'they', I assume you mean Bennett and Robin? I thought she was the coroner. Was she interrogating you?"

"She's the coroner, forensics technician, and

part-time detective when she's not kissing up to Chris."

"Oh. I thought you two were friends."

Kelly emptied her glass and waved at the barmaid for another. "I did, too. Now I see she was just using me to get to Chris. And the fool doesn't even realize she's using him to further her career." She set her glass down and turned her attention toward me. Her gray eyes were mesmerizing.

"Robin told Chris my gun had been fired recently, so they came to my house with several other deputies and asked if I'd mind if they took a look around." Her eyes grew larger and more beautiful. "Look around. Why didn't he say search the place? It's what he meant."

"I assume they didn't find what they were looking for, or you wouldn't be here. Did they tell you what it was?"

"No, but I can guess. Probably wire cutters to cut bailing wire, or maybe one of those fold-up ladders you see on TV. We never found a ladder in the barn, so they probably think Cramer's killer brought one with him."

I tried to recall the scene when I'd found the second body. I couldn't remember seeing a ladder either, which was strange, considering the barn had a loft. It made me wonder how anyone managed to get up there without a ladder."

Kelly disrupted my memory search when she continued. "Anyway, I might not be able to prove my innocence, so I'm hoping I can count on you for help."

"Of course you can, but what's stopping you?"

"Robin can't do ballistic testing, so she sent the gun and bullet from Grace's brain to the lab in Jefferson City. If the results come back positive, I'll be sitting in a cell waiting for my trial." She wanted to say more, but our waitress returned with a glass of wine and a coffee pot.

I waited until we were alone again. "Are you telling me your gun will be a match?" I tried not to let my doubt of her innocence show, but I'm sure my shaking head gave me away.

"Maybe," she said, moving closer. "My service handgun has been jamming, so I switched over to my personal Glock after Amanda returned it. I'd lent it to her right after her father had been killed. She gave it back Saturday. The night Uncle Al and Grace were killed."

I felt my mouth open wider than a dentist's dream. "You think Amanda killed them? Why would she do that?"

She reached for my hands and held them tightly. "No, but I wouldn't put it past her ex. His rap sheet includes armed robbery and battery. Murder is usually the next step. He probably borrowed it from her nightstand, or kitchen drawer, or wherever she left it and forgot it."

"But if they're divorced, how did he get into her house?"

Kelly forced a smile. "Women do get lonely and need a man now and then, Jake. He's one of those guys who can charm a snake. It's hard to turn away a guy that could be on the cover of *Hunk*. I've come so close to falling for his BS myself."

"Ah, I wouldn't know, but I *do* know only psychopaths kill without a motive. Why would he want your uncle and girlfriend dead?"

Kelly tightened her grip on my hands. "It's why I may need you. If it turns out my Glock matches the bullet from Grace, I'll be locked up. None of our people have the experience solving murders that you have, so please tell me you'll follow through, and if it's not him, that you'll find out who did it."

Kelly didn't say much more besides repeat what she'd already said by the time she finished several more glasses of wine. I excused myself to go the men's room because of too much coffee, and she was ready to leave when I returned. It took some talking before I convinced her to give me her keys, but she finally agreed that a DUI, or worse, was the last thing she needed right then.

"You're such a gentleman, Jake. Are you sure you won't come in for a nightcap?" she said after I walked her to her door.

I've been called a lot of things, but a gentleman's never been one of them. Any other time I'd have jumped at the chance for a nightcap with a beautiful, single woman, even if it was only coffee, but Kelly was looking like she'd be spending the night at the throne, so I kissed her gently and took my leave.

Chapter 19

Working with my hands has always helped me think, so the first task I decided to tackle on the old farmhouse the next morning was the roof. I couldn't get Kelly out of my mind. On one hand, I wanted to believe she was being framed, but after sleeping on it, her explanation of how her gun could be the murder weapon seemed a little far-fetched. If she had loaned it to Amanda, then it was more likely Amanda killed Grace, but I had a gut feeling that had been a lie. Kelly hated Grace for the way she'd treated Al, which made Kelly the prime suspect, but I did promise I'd look into Amanda's ex. I wasn't one to go back on my promises and told myself I'd have to drop everything if Kelly were arrested. In the meantime, I needed to get to work on the farm before Jon took over.

It nearly put Bonnie in cardiac arrest when I called the local lumber stores for the price of shingles. The big box stores in Sedalia weren't much better, so I searched all the nearby Craigslist sites and found a roofer in Windsor who was going out of business and had more than enough shingles for our needs that he'd sell at half price. I'd have preferred buying them from a roofing supply that would load them on the roof rather than chance using a flatbed trailer Cramer had left in the barn, but Margot threatened to send Jonathan back if I couldn't handle it. That meant I'd have to hope the trailer's tires didn't blow out, and if they did manage to make it back in one piece, I'd have to carry the shingles up a ladder.

We were going through Lincoln on our way to Windsor, and I'd been thinking of the old tractor in the barn that had come with the farm. It would be a godsend if I could use it to help load the shingles. Bonnie woke me from my deep thoughts with a jab from her elbow. "That's Benson's car! What's he doing at the antique store?"

"I assume that's a rhetorical question—unless you think I'm psychic."

"Pull over, Jake. He's getting something from his trunk. I want to see what it is."

I pulled into the parking lot of a deserted restaurant across the street from the antique store before Bonnie had a chance to elbow me again. I quickly put my phone into camera mode and not a minute too soon. Benson was bent over, rummaging in the trunk of his car, then stopped, stood up straight, and began to look around as if he was checking to see if anyone was watching. We both turned away when he looked in our direction. He must not have seen us, because a second later, he removed something from the trunk about the size and shape of a spare tire, and headed for the front door of the store.

Bonnie turned and looked at me wide-eyed. "Is that what I think it is?"

"If you're thinking it's his spare, my answer is no. That place is an antique store, not a tire shop. And who do you know that wraps their spare tire in a blanket?" I answered, starting the Jeep and pulling back onto the road.

"No, silly. Not the tire or whatever it is—the blanket!"

I turned to give her the Goober look I'd learned from watching *The Andy Griffith Show* as a kid. "Yeah, I saw the blanket, so what…" Then it hit me. "It's just like the others. Isn't it?"

"Way to go, Sherlock. Shouldn't we wait until he comes back out?" she asked, straining her neck to watch the antique store as I drove on.

"And let him see us? No, I don't think that's wise. Besides the guy in Windsor expected us fifteen minutes ago," I said, handing her my cell phone.

"Why don't you zoom in on the pictures I took and make sure the blanket's the same?"

I took a quick glance in my side view mirror to get one last look at Benson's car, then looked over at Bonnie, who was punching her finger at the last picture I'd taken. "Use your thumb and index finger, Bon. The only thing you'll manage that way is to put a hole in my screen."

She put the phone down, but not before giving me a dirty look. "Polaroids were a lot simpler."

Neither one of us spoke until we were within a mile from Windsor. The guy we were supposed to meet didn't live in town, and I'd missed the crossroad with the blue house and white fence he told me to look for. I knew better than to ask Bonnie to look it up on Google Maps with my phone, so I pulled over to do it myself.

"Google, show me 1356 Grasscreek..." Fred decided to say hello to a couple Guernsey cows that had come up to the fence where I had parked before I could finish telling Google the address. Google came back with a map of someplace in New York. I have no idea what Fred said to the cows. For that matter, I wasn't even sure if they were Guernseys, but I was pretty sure we weren't in New York City.

"It's back about a mile, Jake," Bonnie said before

I could tell Fred to quit barking at the cows. She was pointing to a map she had pulled out of I know not where and had a huge grin on her face. "Sometimes the old ways are a lot better," she added, shoving the map in my lap. Fred stopped barking and turned to see what Bonnie had given me—I swear he was smiling.

"So now you read maps?" I asked, ruffling his fur.

"Of course I can read a map. Didn't I tell you I worked as a cartographer before I went into teaching?"

"I meant, Fred, Bon," I said and began to turn the Jeep around, forgetting I was pulling a trailer. The road was too narrow to make the turn without backing up and when I did, I heard the shattering of plastic as the trailer jackknifed into the rear of the Jeep.

Bonnie looked like one of those wide-eyed cartoon characters. "What was that?"

"I think I jackknifed the trailer," I said jumping out of the Jeep to check out the damage.

Luckily, it was only a broken tail light. I had stopped before the trailer put a dent in the fender. That soon became the least of my worries. In my haste to check on the damage, I'd left my door open, and Fred had decided to visit his new found friends. He was over at the fence, barking at the cows, and a semi-truck loaded with live chickens was speeding down the road toward us. The driver of the truck slammed on his brakes and started to slide sideways when he saw the Jeep blocking the road. Bonnie was still in the passenger seat where she was about to become part of a chicken sandwich.

Chapter 20

Some people claim to see their entire life flash by in the millisecond before a fatal accident. All I saw in my mind's eye was Bonnie and Fred being hit by a semi load of chickens before I jumped into action and hopped back into the driver's seat. I threw the Jeep in drive while flooring it without bothering close the door. I managed to get off the road and onto the shoulder as the semi went sliding by. Fortunately, the Jeep's door closed on its own because of the sudden jerk forward or it would have been covered in chicken blood and feathers—the semi missed us by inches.

I got out of the Jeep again, called Fred over to my side, and watched as the semi straightened out and pulled to a stop at the side of the road. Bonnie decided to join us when the driver of the truck got out of his cab and started to walk toward us. He had a sawed-off baseball bat in his right hand that he kept slapping into his left hand. The guy didn't look tough, but I knew I was no match for the baseball bat.

Without thinking, I stepped in front of Bonnie and Fred.

"Who's the idiot that decided to turn around at the bottom of a dip in the road?" he asked when he got close enough to talk, but not yet close enough to swing his bat. The driver looked like he had eaten at too many truck stops. I wondered how he managed to get behind the wheel of his truck and still be able to turn it. He made sumo wrestlers look like starving ballerinas.

Bonnie stepped in front of me before I could own up to my stupidity. "If you weren't going like a bat out of hell, you would have had plenty of time to stop," she said, shaking a fist at him. Then Fred decided he wanted to put his two cents in too and started growling.

"Whoa, you two," I said, stepping between them and the truck driver. I turned toward him and added. "I'm the idiot, sir."

Now that he was close enough to wield his bat, I thought about how I'd disarm him if he did. Not only was he fat, he was short, too. I was also a hundred pounds lighter and six inches taller and had the advantage of being ten years younger.

"Well, you nearly caused me to turn my rig on its side. What the hell were you thinking?"

I could see the muscles in his arm relax as he

backed up a few steps. "I guess I wasn't thinking. I should've realized someone coming over the hill wouldn't see us soon enough if they were speeding."

"He's the one who needs to apologize, Jake." Bonnie must have also realized the fight had left him. "We should call that chicken plant he works for."

The driver's grip on his bat tightened and his eyes narrowed. "It'd be my word against yours."

"No one's calling anybody," I said, cutting Bonnie off before she could dig a deeper hole. "I said I was sorry, so let's move on, okay?"

The truck driver forced a smile. "Yeah. No harm, no foul," he said and turned to go back to his truck.

"Do you know how to get to Grasscreek Drive?" Bonnie asked before he'd gone two steps. Her tone suggested she had accepted the truce.

The driver turned back to her, smiling and resting the bat on his shoulder. "That's why you did the U-turn?"

"It's supposed to intersect with this road, but we missed it. Bonnie's map says we passed it a mile back, but I never saw a street sign," I answered.

"Or the blue barn and white fence," Bonnie added.

The driver laughed. "That's cuz you ain't passed it yet. You can't see no barn till you get over the rise in the road I just come over."

"But the maps says we passed it," Bonnie said.

"And probably drawn by some college gradgeeate who never come close to here. I'm telling you, it's just over the hill. You'll see an old Ford 8N just before you get to the fence."

He shook his head, muttered something we couldn't hear, and continued toward his truck. "And I'd find a better place to turn around if I was you. The next driver may not be as good as me."

We finally found a safe place to turn around about a mile out of our way. I could see by the way Bonnie kept pulling at a non-existent earring that her mind was in overdrive. "What's a Ford 8N, Jake? Is that some kind of SUV or something?"

"It's a tractor. They were very popular back in the forties and fifties."

She stopped pulling at her earlobe and looked at me with wide eyes. "How do you know that, mister know-it-all?"

"Because that's the model tractor in your barn. I did some research on it when I couldn't get it to turn over. Good thing I did too or I might have burned something up trying to jump it with the battery charger on the workbench."

Bonnie gave me the "tell someone who cares"

look. "I'll remember that for next time I talk to my bridge club. I'm sure it'll put a few of them to sleep long enough to outbid them."

I was dying to tell her all about the difference between positive and negative grounding systems but didn't want to contribute to her devious bridge tactics. "Well, I for one am glad I didn't burn out the starter or I wouldn't be able to use the bucket when I have to load your shingles."

"Will it go that high?"

"I think so. Cramer must have used it to load hay in the barn's loft, so it should…"

"Should what, Jake?"

I slowed down and pulled over to the side of the road. Revelations come to me few and far between, and I didn't want to be distracted from driving when I told her. I needed to see her reaction. "That's how they hung Cramer, Bon, with the tractor's bucket."

She shook her head from side to side. "For this, you had to pull over? I fail to see how this helps. I'm sure Kelly already guessed the murderer used the tractor."

"No she didn't, and there are no ladders or hay elevators in the barn, so it had to have been the tractor. And only someone who knows something about these old tractors could have done it."

Bonnie looked at me with her mouth half-open,

but no words came out.

"It's the voltage and polarity, Bon. You have to jump the battery to get it started and only someone who knew about the 8N would know it has positive grounding and a six-volt battery. That, someone, had to be another farmer, and what farmer do we know who hated Cramer enough to kill him?"

"The nosy neighbor?" she asked as I pulled the Jeep back on the road.

Fred wanted out by the time I found the roofer. We had left the pavement behind us once I turned on Grasscreek and the noise of gravel hitting the undercarriage had woken him. I got out and opened his door, and he shot off to the nearest tree.

Bonnie walked over to me and whispered, "I think you should offer him less than half."

"Why's that, Bon?"

"Look at this dump. He could start his own junkyard with all these broken washing machines, rusted cars, and building materials. I'll bet he got most of those materials off of job sites and he'd be willing to take anything he can get for them."

"Whoa, Bon. We better turn around right now if there's any chance they're hot."

"Bout time you got here," the roofer said, joining us from out of nowhere. "Y'all get lost?" He looked to be in his early thirties or late twenties. It was hard to tell because of the untrimmed, rust-colored beard covering most of his face. I could tell he was the real deal by the holes in his jeans at the knees. I remember seeing roofers with the same holes when I had worked for a roofing company in my teens. Back then, there were two ways to lay shingles: sitting down or kneeling—evidently, he was a kneeler.

"Yeah, I missed the white fence with the yellow balloons," I answered, trying to keep a straight face as I offered my hand. "I'm Jake, and this here is my good friend, Bonnie Jones, who needs the shingles."

The roofer wiped his hand on his dirty jeans before shaking mine. "I don't remember saying nothing about no balloons."

"Jake's being a wise guy," Bonnie said, putting her hand behind her back and out of reach of the roofer's dirty mitt. "Can you show us the shingles?"

He spit out the tobacco he'd been chewing and started walking toward an old pole barn that should have been torn down years ago. "Ya bet. Got 'em right over here."

Fred joined us before we got to the barn. His legs and feet were covered in mud. I took one look at him and started to shake my head, but didn't have time to scold him. It was my own fault for letting him wander. Just about all these farms had ponds, and I never knew a Golden Retriever who was able to avoid open water. In turn for not being scolded, he decided to share some of his treasure and brushed up against my legs. Our roofer didn't seem to notice and didn't slow down for a second.

Once we got closer, I realized I'd been mistaken in thinking the building was a barn. It didn't have four walls and a door but was completely open at one end. I believe it's what farmers call a machine shed. The shed was filled with more junk and pallets stacked with roofing material of every color and type imaginable. He had three-tab shingles, architectural shingles, cedar shakes, clay and cement tiles, and even roll roofing. I also saw several stacks of metal roofing, both new and used.

When we caught up to the roofer, he was standing by a stack of three-tab shingles. "Them here's the ones I put on Craigslist," he said, taking another pinch of chewing tobacco.

Fred started barking at me before I could ask about the ownership of the shingles. He left my side and went over to a pallet in the far corner. "Not now, Freddie," I said.

He barked again, then ran over to me, barked, then ran back to whatever he'd found.

The roofer pushed his chew between his teeth and cheek and laughed. "Guess he wants a blanket.

I'd be willing to throw one in if ya buy the shingles."

"Jake, you better come here." Bonnie had gone over to see what Fred had found, so I did as she said and joined them. Fred's pallet was stacked with blankets wrapped in clear plastic bags. They all had the same pattern as Tigger's blanket.

"Where'd you get these?" I shouted out to the roofer who had stayed back with the shingles.

"Same place I get most my stuff. At auctions. I think that one come from one I went to in Lincoln a couple months ago." The roofer scratched his tobacco-stained beard. "I'd of had both pallets, but Mike Anderson outbid me on the other one. Mike's about as much an antique dealer as me. I bet he ain't got one antique in the whole store. All I ever seen him buy was junk and surplus goods."

I grabbed a blanket the same color as Tigger's and walked back to the shingles. "Looks like you have a deal. I'll take fifteen squares of the three-tabs and this blanket. You *do* have a forklift to load them, I hope."

Chapter 21

Fred had his big head resting on the front bench seat with his rear firmly planted on the back seat. Bonnie was giving him a head massage as a reward for having found the blankets. "I still don't understand how the blankets tie it all together, Jake." She was turned toward me, holding Fred's head with both hands.

"Simple, Ms. Watson. We now know Fitzgerald knew Anderson and Benson. Isn't it obvious they were all in it together?"

Bonnie quit massaging Fred's head and looked at me with a blank stare. "Together in what: grave robbing or murder?"

Fred showed his displeasure and tried to get Bonnie to resume her massage by sticking his big snout under her right hand.

"Probably both, but I won't know for sure for a couple days."

I was about ready to turn onto Highway 65 and

heard Fred thumping his tail against the rear seat. I couldn't look, but I knew by the sound that Bonnie had resumed the massage.

"Would you care to enlighten those of us who can't read minds just how you'll know?" she asked.

"I'm going to take a page from the NSA's dirty tricks book and tap Benson's cell phone."

I was merging into traffic and still couldn't see her reaction, but I could imagine her mouth was wide open while she stared at me like I'd finally lost it when my phone rang.

"Can you get that, Bon?" Another chicken truck was coming down the road, and I didn't need the distraction of my cell phone.

Bonnie knew enough to put it in speaker mode before answering. "Hello, Jake? It's Sheriff Bennett." His tone told me he hadn't called to chat about fishing.

"Hi, Sheriff, what can I do for you?"

He cleared his throat before answering. "Kelly wanted me to call. She said to tell you she needs you to do what you and she discussed last night, whatever that is." He paused, presumably waiting for me to tell him what she must not have. "I don't suppose you want to share it with me?"

"Does this mean she's been arrested?" I asked, pulling off to the side of the road and parking.

He paused again, but not as long as before. "I'm sorry, Jake. I know you two have become close, but the lab report came back. It was her gun that killed Grace Wilson."

"But she lent it to Amanda and didn't get it back until after the murder. Shouldn't you be arresting Amanda instead?"

"It's her word against Amanda's, and Amanda denies ever having the gun. Sorry, Jake, but I've got to go. Let me know what it is she wants you to do, and maybe I can help."

Bennett disconnected, and I looked over at Bonnie who had heard the entire conversation. She didn't have to say a word—her face told me everything. She sat with her mouth open, exposing her missing bottom dentures.

"What does she want you to do, Jake?" she asked when she found her voice.

"She thought Amanda's ex might have taken the gun she lent to Amanda," I answered, pulling out into traffic.

"Except now we know that's a smokescreen. She lied about giving the gun to Amanda. I'm sorry, Jake, but your girlfriend is looking pretty guilty."

"Or Amanda's lying."

Bonnie raised her left eyebrow and made some kind of sarcastic laugh. "Why would she do that? She was never a suspect, was she?"

"No, but her ex was. I suspect protecting him comes before protecting Kelly. Now I need that spyware more than ever."

It took several tries before I found the perfect spyware. I reasoned that after I tested it on Benson, I could use it to spy on Amanda and her ex. Kelly might not like it, but Amanda looked like the real suspect. Why else would she have denied having the gun? On the other hand, why would she hide the sword she bought from the antique dealer where we could find it?

I didn't want to compromise my own phone, so a smartphone app was not an option. I wanted a PC program I knew I could delete without leaving any trace of my illegal activity, even if it meant installing a new hard drive. Most of the programs I found required the user to install an app on the phone to be spied on. Those were the ones made for parents who wanted to keep an eye on their teens. I knew there had to something out there equivalent to what our government uses—something that would let us do our dirty deed without the user's knowledge, and I found it after only a couple hours of searching and testing.

Bonnie looked like might pop an artery when I

showed her Benson's call logs. She'd come down to the kitchen for a nightcap and decided to join me at the table to see what progress I'd made. I'd been at it so long that Fred had fallen asleep under the table with Tigger curled up next to him.

"And he doesn't know you're spying on him?" she asked after taking another sip of her Jack Daniels. "Not according to the makers of the spyware," I answered.

She adjusted her reading glasses and took a closer look at the list. "Wow, I can't believe that'd be possible. Shouldn't somebody shut them down?"

"Not without a cruise missile, and that would start World War Three—the site's in Russia. But that's not our problem, Bon. Look at all those calls to Fitzgerald. Notice anything about the last one?"

"March fourth. That's two days before you found him in the cemetery."

"Exactly. I wish Benson had texted him. I can read those but voice isn't recorded."

Bonnie smiled sarcastically. "You're telling me the KGB is no match for our NSA? I hear they record everything we say on the phone."

"I believe your KGB is called the FSB now, and I doubt if they use this software. I'm sure theirs is far more sophisticated."

"Whatever, Jake. My point is that we still have

no proof Benson or his buddy Anderson killed Cramer. And we have less proof they killed his crazy neighbors."

I didn't bother to remark on the logic of having less than nothing. I'd known Bonnie long enough to know not to argue with her when she had Jack Daniels backing her up.

"Oh, I don't think any of them killed Cramer. All I'm saying is the blankets connect them, and the phone logs prove that. It looks like Benson was the fence for Fitzgerald, and he sold some of his loot to Anderson, including Captain Scott's stuff. We also know from Fitzgerald's wife and Anderson's son, what's his name—Jared, that Amanda was having an affair with Fitzgerald."

She emptied the last of her Jack Daniels into her glass. "I don't recall Jared saying that."

Ordinarily, she'd be able to follow my logic, but it was getting late and the bourbon didn't help either. "When he called her a cougar. He must have known about her affair with Fitzgerald. What I don't understand is why she bought the sword and knife from Anderson." I didn't mention I'd planned to use the spyware on Amanda and her ex.

As if she knew what I was thinking, Bonnie drained her glass, reached under the table for her cat, and headed for the stairs. "I'm going back to bed, and if you're thinking of spying on Amanda, I suggest you get to work on the roof first before Margot sends Jon out to do it."

Bonnie had hit a nerve with her remark about the roof. The snow from Sunday had melted, so I thought I'd better at least check out the tractor to see if I'd be able to use it to load the shingles. I waited for her bedroom door to close, then headed for the barn with my shadow at my heels. Tapping Amanda's phone and her ex's would have to wait.

To my amazement, the old tractor started on the first turn of the key after I hooked up the battery charger and set it to six volts. I had expected a sixty-seven-year-old engine to be a bit more cantankerous. Cramer must have taken good care of his equipment.

Just as I raised the bucket to its limit to see if it would go high enough to load shingles on a roof, the old tractor coughed and died. Looks like I'd spoken too soon about Cramer's penchant for maintenance.

"Let's go back inside, and warm up, Fred. This can wait until tomorrow."

Fred had wandered off to the back of the barn where I couldn't see him. When he didn't come when called, I tried shining my flashlight in his direction. Although the light was dim, I could see him scratching at a big box. How I envied his thick coat and ability to ward off the cold air. "Come on, Fred, or I'll lock up and leave you here all night."

I barely made it to the barn doors when I heard him at my heels.

Wednesday morning found Fred and me alone with Tigger, and without transportation. Bonnie had found a church her first week in town and left for Bible study before I got up. My previous night of spying on Benson and checking out the tractor had kept me up past my bedtime, so Bonnie didn't wake me to go with her. Or maybe she didn't want me sharing the cold I'd picked up with the rest of the congregation. Not that I had any intention of joining her. What I wanted was her Jeep so I could visit Kelly. I thought about driving the tractor to church and trading rides but quickly dismissed that idea. I doubt if it had a top speed faster than a three-legged mule with blinders, and something told me Bonnie might forget where she was and tell me where I could stick the tractor.

Fred and Tigger lacked the social skills to carry on a conversation over breakfast, so the three of us ate breakfast in near silence. It didn't surprise me when Tigger ignored my attempt to make breakfast, but when Fred turned his nose up at my burnt toast, I began to wish I'd waited for Bonnie. I'd utter an occasional comment to Fred because he pretended to listen. Tigger, on the other hand, acted like I didn't exist. She even refused the scraps of bacon I'd throw her way, acting like I'd tried to poison her. Fred had no such qualms. Unlike the toast, he didn't care how it was cooked, and he caught his before it hit the ground then took hers.

After breakfast, we headed toward the barn. It was time to get the tractor working and load the roof. Fred was the first out the door with Tigger right behind. I'd thought about going back to bed but knew Bonnie's threat about Jon was real. I'd become dependent on Margot's paychecks and didn't feel like sharing them with her son—my bills back in Colorado still needed to be paid, whether I was there or not.

Our trio soon became a duo when Tigger took off for the loft, hot on some critter's trail. I think Fred wanted to join the cat, but despite being several years older, he hadn't learned to climb. Fred soon forgot about Tigger and followed his nose to the far side of the barn, while I went over to check on the tractor that had died on me the previous night.

As a kid growing up I'd worked on a lot of cars built before they had sensors and computers that we didn't know we needed to control the fuel, oxygen, ignition and a hundred other things. My father used to tell me there were only two things needed to make them run; gas and spark. I decided to start with the fuel and quickly realized why the tractor had died. It had run out of gas. There was a fuel cutoff switch that had been set to off. I also noticed the bucket wasn't where I'd left it. There must be a slow leak somewhere in the hydraulic system I'd need to check out, so I switched on the gas, pulled out the choke and tried to start the motor. It took a bit to get gas back into the carburetor, but the old gal finally fired up and I raised the bucket again to make sure it still worked.

Fred heard the tractor and came back to see what all the noise was about. He sat on his haunches, smiling. "What are you grinning at?" I asked.

He barked, then got up and started slowly walking back toward the rear of the barn where he'd been the night before. When I didn't get off the tractor, he stopped and barked again. I knew him well enough to know he found something and wanted me to follow, so I got off the tractor and did as he asked. "This better be good, Freddie. You know I need to get started on those shingles before Bonnie gets back from church."

I was no sooner off the tractor and following Fred when I heard tiny footsteps behind me. "Find anything tasty up in the loft, Tigger?" I said, turning around. Tigger stopped following and sat down to preen her fur, acting like she had no idea what I'd just said. I didn't have time to play cat and mouse with her, so I went back to see what Fred had found that was so interesting. Tigger waited a few seconds, then resumed tailing me.

"Okay, so you found another cedar chest like the one Bonnie found in the attic." Fred wasn't bred to point, but he did the best he could to show me his find. By the way, it was constructed with a maple veneer and cross-sawn inlays on the front, I guessed it to be from the early sixties. I remember my father buying something similar at a second-hand store for my sister. She had called it her hope chest.

"Whatever's in there could no longer be edible, Fred. By the looks of the dust on the lid, that chest hasn't been opened in twenty years."

Fred ignored me and went over and scratched at the lid. Tigger, I noticed, had perched herself on a nearby bale of hay, watching us. Maybe she thought Fred had found her a nest of mice and was waiting for someone to open it for her. Not wanting to disappoint either of them, I tried to oblige, only to find it locked. There was a simple lock on the front of the chest that any kid with a bobby pin could open in thirty seconds. Unfortunately, I was neither a kid nor did I have a bobby pin. It took me several minutes to pop it open with my trusty, Swiss army knife.

Fred started wagging his tail and Tigger jumped off her perch to run toward the front of the barn. "What are you doing back there, Jake?" Bonnie had returned.

"Fred found what looks like Amanda's teenage hope chest. She must have forgotten it was here. It looks like it hasn't been opened in years."

Bonnie tilted her head to one side, looking at the chest, and turned to Fred "Your master wouldn't be blaming you for his nosiness, would he?"

"Good one, Bon. Really, it was Fred who found it. He must have thought there was something good to eat in there because he wouldn't leave me alone until I opened it."

Bonnie shuffled closer while reaching for the glasses she kept on a rope around her neck. "I doubt that," she said, shaking her head and wrinkling her nose after looking into the chest.

"What? That it's her hope chest or that there's something good to eat?"

"Both."

"Why's that, Bon?"

"Well, if it wasn't for your cold, you wouldn't be asking if whatever stinks in there is good to eat. Then there's the Miss Me jeans on top. They both suggest someone's been in the chest recently. If it was Amanda, she would have taken it like she did the other one."

"Miss Me jeans? What are those?"

Bonnie raised her eyebrows making her wrinkles look like an old-fashioned washboard. "It's a brand of jeans that didn't exist when Amanda was a teenager. And the stench you can't smell is something dead."

It was my turn to wrinkle my nose, trying to get a whiff of whatever had died, but all I could do was sneeze. "Hmm, now that you mention it, I do smell something," I lied and started removing items from the chest.

"My God, Jake. Is that a Confederate flag?"

Under MissMe were the remains of a Confederate flag. It must have been covering Captain Scott's casket, by the looks of it. Someone had put what the worms hadn't eaten into a clear plastic bag like the ones used for good blankets. "I believe so." I set the bag aside and kept digging to see if there were any more stolen relics inside.

Chapter 22

"Well, Jake, if you're not going to read the diary, I will." We had taken the hope chest back to the house, so we could get a better look at its contents. Bonnie's face had a huge smile when I removed a box of old pictures and a girl's diary. I'd assumed the diary had been owned by a girl because of its pink cover, but I didn't mention it to Bonnie for fear she'd call me a chauvinist. I'd also removed a dried up mouse from the bottom that must have fallen in when the owner was rearranging things. Evidently, she hadn't seen him sneak in—then again, maybe she had—and shut the lid on him out of fright. Either way, it was a death sentence for the rodent.

"This diary is twenty years old, Bon. I don't see how reading it will help find Cramer's killer."

She grabbed the diary from my hand and put it in her lap where it would be safe for the time being. "I thought you said it was the nosey neighbor because it had to be someone who knew about old tractors and

Polaroids."

Her misunderstanding of my earlier explanation brought a smile to my face. "Polarity, Bon. Polaroids are something else altogether."

"Whatever, smarty, but aren't you forgetting Margot? She's not paying you to solve another murder."

"I promised Kelly I'd get to the bottom of the murders, Bon. I can't break that promise."

She picked up the diary and tried to open it. "You also promised Margot to fix the farm," she said while trying to force the lock on the diary.

"Do you want Kelly to hang for a murder she didn't commit?"

Bonnie frowned. "They don't hang people anymore. Not even in Missouri. Besides, how do you know she didn't do it? Didn't ballistics prove it was her gun?"

"Yes. It's why Bennett arrested her. I know all the evidence points to her. I think I'm the only one who believes she didn't do it. How about I work on the roof while I try to figure this out? I'm sure Margot will be happy to hear Fred found her husband's great-grandfather's flag. Maybe that'll give me the time I need."

Bonnie shook her head, not up and down in concurrence, but slowly from side to side the way one does when they don't agree. "No sense in arguing with a man in love. I'll tell Margot you're working on the roof, but you better get to the bottom of it soon, or Jon will be here before you know it."

I reached for the diary and snapped open the lock before handing it back. "Thanks, Bon. If you don't mind reading it to see who wrote it and why it's here, I can get back to my surveillance of Amanda and her ex. The more eyes we have on this, the sooner I can prove Kelly's innocent and get back to working on the roof."

She put the diary back in her lap and smiled. "On one condition, Jake."

"Oh?"

"Buy me lunch first. Someone at church said there's a great barbecue joint in town."

Bonnie's church friend must have been talking about another town. I ordered a pulled pork sandwich and Bonnie chose the special of the day, the beef brisket. I think it must have been last week's special because she started to get sick before we were halfway home. Fred didn't seem to mind my sandwich, but there was no way I wanted to see dog poop all over the house, so Bonnie's leftovers went into the trash. Fortunately, Bonnie was better house-trained and knew how to use the toilet.

Even without Bonnie's diarrhea and my lingering cold, loading the roof was out of the question; I needed to see Kelly. I made up an excuse that the half-inch of snow we had on Sunday hadn't melted because the sun didn't shine on the north side of the roof. I told Bonnie I had no intention of trying the roof as a ski jump, and it could wait until tomorrow.

Sheriff Bennett made an exception to his visiting hours, and let me see Kelly. I was led to a room and told to wait after being searched for weapons. I'd seen movies where prisoners and their guests were separated by glass and had to talk over an intercom, so it surprised me when they led me into what must be their interrogation room. Kelly was brought in a few minutes later by a female deputy I vaguely recognized. She waited until her handcuffs were removed, and then came over to me and gave me a huge hug.

"Thank you for seeing me, Jake," she said after she released me. She was still beautiful, despite the lack of makeup and unwashed hair.

I followed her lead and sat opposite her at the small table after the deputy left us. "Bennett tells me your gun tested positive. We both know you didn't do it, so like it or not, it looks like Amanda's setting you up. Do you have any idea why she would do that?"

She shook her head slowly back and forth. "She must be protecting her ex. I know she still loves him and was hoping they could get back together, but I didn't think she'd let me hang to save his sorry ass."

I held back the urge to repeat what Bonnie had said about hanging. "Is this room wired, Kell?"

She stared at me like I'd been the one who just swore, then wet her lips, and leaned in closer. "You know something that can help me, Jake?"

"Maybe, but it's between you and me."

"Shoot. We use a tape recorder when we interrogate suspects, so whatever you say is between us."

I proceeded to tell her about the spyware I'd found and how I planned to use it on Amanda and her ex. Then I brought her up to date about the connection between Fitzgerald, Benson, and Anderson. I finished with how the kid from the antique store had told me Amanda bought the sword.

"Are you sure, Jake," she asked once I rested my jaws.

"He sold it to that cougar on TV. Those were his exact words."

She leaned back and seemed to be digesting everything I'd said. "Are you sure he wasn't talking about the reporter, Carla Kennedy?"

"Positive. Carla had no reason to buy the sword, and I wouldn't exactly call her a cougar. Of course, Amanda had no reason to buy it either. If she'd been having an affair with Fitzgerald, wouldn't he have just given it to her?"

"They weren't the only women on that broadcast, Jake. I like to think teenage boys still think of me as a cougar."

I felt my own eyes enlarge. "You were on the broadcast?"

She chuckled. "Yes. Robin and I were there as well. Didn't you notice me?"

"I must have been too focused on Cramer. I thought he'd shot at me and Fred the night before, but you already know that." I paused for a second to think of anything I'd missed. My time must be running out. "Oh, I forgot to tell you what Fred found in the barn today."

Bennett stuck his head into the room before I could say more. He avoided looking at Kelly and addressed me. "Five more minutes, Jake."

He gave Kelly a pained look as he closed the door.

Kelly stared at the door for a few moments before asking me to tell her about Fred's barn find.

"It's a hope chest. I doubt if it belonged to

Amanda. She had one in the attic and took it with her after she sold the house. Bonnie's going through it as we speak."

Her face lit up. It was only a spark, but it was enough to wash away her depression for a few seconds. "I'd all but forgotten about that. I put a bunch of stuff in Amanda's barn a couple years ago after my mother died and I'd cleaned out her house. I haven't seen it since."

I nearly fell over as I pushed back in my chair "It's your chest, Kell?"

"Uh-huh. Why, did you read my diary?"

"No, I didn't read it." I didn't mention Bonnie was probably reading it at that very moment. "But we found a flag that I'm pretty sure came from Captain Scott's grave. We also found a dead mouse who couldn't be more than a few weeks old."

She let out a small sigh. "Then Amanda's been in there. I haven't seen that chest since I stored it."

Her remark caught me off guard and I jerked my head back. "Amanda? Why not her father or the nosy neighbor?"

She reached out and took both my hands in hers. "Was it locked when you found it?"

"Yes, but I didn't let that stop me from opening it. Don't worry—I didn't break it."

"Then it had to have been her. She's the only

one who knows the key was taped under the chest. It was locked, Jake."

I started to tell her that I never saw a key when I moved the chest into the house, but Bennett returned all too soon and terminated my visit before I could ask her any more questions. He didn't even give me a chance to hug her before making me leave.

"I wonder if I could ask a favor, Sheriff," I said after we left the interrogation room and he was unlocking the door to the lobby.

Bennett shifted his weight from his left foot to his right and crossed his arms. "The last time you asked that we had three murders. Come to think of it, we haven't had a murder since…since until now."

I tried to smile, but it came off more as a smirk. "It's not for me, Sheriff. It's for Kelly."

He uncrossed his arms and rubbed imaginary stubble on his chin. "What do you need, Jake?"

"Can you give me a copy of the ballistics report?"

"Why do you want that? I hope you're not meddling in my case again."

I cleared my throat and spoke with the most convincing voice I could muster. "Just trying to help, Sheriff. We both know Kelly didn't murder Grace Wilson, and I need to see all the evidence against her if I'm going to help her. If you want to call that meddling, so be it, but you should look at it as a free consultation. After all, I do have more experience solving murders than all of your deputies put together."

Bennett looked at me like I'd just used a four-letter word, then his expression softened. "I'll email you a copy, and don't think for one minute this gives you a license to stick your nose where it's not wanted. I'm only doing it for Kelly."

I wanted to thank him by shaking his hand, but I'd been scratching a rash lately. If I'd picked up poison ivy from my adventures on the farm, the last thing I needed was to give it to the sheriff.

Fred was still up and happy to see me when I got back to the farm. I wanted to tell Bonnie about my meeting with Kelly, but she and Tigger were upstairs in her bedroom. I didn't want to disturb her for fear she was sleeping. It was too early for me to hit the sack and I wouldn't be able to sleep if I did. I was halfway through making a pot of coffee when I remembered I hadn't eaten.

"Want to visit your favorite restaurant, Freddie?" The old farm didn't have Internet, and I wanted to see if Bennett had sent the email. I could have used my smartphone, but my eyes aren't what they used to be, and reading a detailed report on the small screen was out of the question.

Fred barked and wagged his tail. When realization set in, his whole body started wagging. Maybe I imagined that part. Like most parents who tend to think their children are exceptional, I tend to think Fred understands me.

The restaurant was quiet and nearly empty, so I found a seat against the wall, making sure no one could see what I was doing. I had promised Fred I'd get him a couple of plain hamburgers before going inside. Most dogs would have been fine with the cool evening temperature in the low sixties, but most dogs didn't have down under their fur, so I left the windows half-open.

There was no email from Bennett yet, so I started scrolling through some of the news stories displayed on my home page. It made me feel sorry for people who believed some of them. Most of the fake news was political, but I had to laugh when one of the stories showed pictures of a six hundred pound man who had lost four hundred pounds. I might have bought it, but by the looks of the before and after pictures, he'd also lost twenty years and had a hair transplant. Others, like the two-headed cow epidemic, were simply disgusting. I was about ready to sign out when I saw an article on the record sale of a

Confederate battle flag. General J.E.B Stuart's personal battle flag had sold for $956,000, back in 2007.

I clicked on the article and it brought up a picture of the flag. I couldn't believe it—Stuart's flag was in worse shape than the one we'd found in Kelly's hope chest. If hers was worth half as much, it could be a huge motive for murder.

Chapter 23

"How do you expect me to see that, Jake?" Bonnie said when I showed her the picture of General Stuart's battle flag the next morning. She must have been feeling better because she got up before me to let Fred out, and I woke to the smell of fried bacon.

I noticed a rash on her foreman when she gave me back my cell phone. "Does that itch, Bon?" I asked, pointing to her arm, and the tiny blisters that had formed on top of a red rash.

"Is the Pope Catholic?" she answered, scratching it.

"You shouldn't do that, Bon. It'll only make it worse."

She put down her fork and stared at me. "I'm old enough to be your mother, young man, so I don't need no wet-nosed brat telling me how to treat poison ivy. This isn't my first rodeo, you know." She wriggled her nose at me and went back to scratching, only this time she did it with a vengeance.

"Sorry, ma'am." I turned away, trying not to laugh for fear I'd spit out my scrambled eggs. I saw Fred watching my every move when I turned. He must have been waiting for those eggs.

I threw Fred a piece of my bacon and turned back toward Bonnie. "Well, if it makes you feel any better, Bon, I got it, too. I thought I'd picked it up from the entrance to the caretaker's shack—the place is covered with it—but you've barely been out of the house, so maybe you got it from something I touched."

"You can catch poison ivy from someone? I thought that was an old wives' tale."

"Not by touching them. The urushiol oil it secretes can stick to clothing. Maybe I wiped some of the oil on a towel or something."

She started to take a drink of her coffee but stopped with the cup in mid-air. "How do you know this stuff, Jake? I can't remember what a stigma or pistil are supposed to do, let alone the biology of poison ivy."

I reached for her hand and lowered her cup before she spilled it. "The Internet, Bon. I was researching poisons for my work in progress and poison ivy popped up. Sometimes, I think I spend more time researching than writing, given all the blind alleys I follow."

"Right. You saw it on the Internet, so it must be true. I heard that from Abraham Lincoln, in case you're wondering." She smiled and started scratching again.

My cell beeped, notifying me I had a new email. A quick glance told me it was from Bennett. "It's about time." I put my plate down for Fred and threw a small piece of bacon to Tigger who had finally got out of bed to see what was for breakfast. "I've got to make a quick trip to the library, Bon. Do you want to go?" I chose the library instead of the golden arches because hard copy printouts weren't on their menu, and I wanted the ballistics report on paper.

She frowned and shook her head. "No thanks, Jake. Some of us don't have the luxury of reading all day and need to do a little work around here."

"Sorry, Bon, but I'll make it up to you. How about I stop at the store and get us some calamine lotion?"

True to his word, Bennett sent me the ballistics report from Jefferson City as a PDF file. I took a quick look at it and didn't see anything earthshaking, so I sent it to the printer and got ready to leave. I'd left Fred with Bonnie and felt lost without him. The temperature had changed like the locals said it would. It took a bit longer than fifteen minutes, as they say, but at seventy-five degrees, it had become too hot to have left him in the car. Maybe I should buy one of those service dog vests so he could come inside air-conditioned buildings in warm weather.

Before I shut down my computer, something in the report caught my eye. A summary on the last page said the bullet was a match to Kelly's gun, but it also went into detail on the gunpowder and type of oil it had picked up traveling through the barrel. Nowhere did it mention any human DNA. I'd have to read the whole report later that night.

I had to pass the mystery section on my way to the printer and got sidetracked by the indie author section. I just had to see if any of my books were on the shelf. I found several authors I recognized from my Facebook author groups, but none of mine. There were several by Steve Demaree, a few by Deborah Garner, Elise Abram, and Linda Crowder, but the one that made me smile was a book by a distant cousin of mine, Christine Grey. They also had authors I'd never heard of. Judging from the USA Today bestselling banners on the covers, maybe I should have. I wanted to check out a few titles I hadn't read yet but knew I had to get back to work on the roof, and besides, I didn't have a library card.

I was on my way out the door when all of a

sudden I stopped. People coming in thanked me for holding the door open for them not knowing I was in the middle of an epiphany. Out of nowhere, I remembered Amanda had been scratching a rash the day I'd found Al dead in the barn.

I stopped off at the barn to retrieve the Captain's battle flag before going into the house. Although it could be worth a fortune, my plan wasn't to bring it in for safe keeping, but it did call for handling the flag with care, so I went over to the tractor on my way to the hope chest to retrieve the work gloves I'd left on the seat. I picked up my gloves and made a mental note to get some hydraulic fluid, as the lift cylinders had leaked and created a small puddle.

I put on the gloves and proceeded to the hope chest. With a huge sigh of relief, I saw the flag was where we'd left it. Whoever had put it there either didn't know its worth or was dead. I hoped for the former, or my theory was as dead as the stiffs in the family cemetery.

I gently removed the flag from the chest. Although I treated the flag with the respect it deserved by being gentle, that wasn't why I'd put on the gloves. If my theory was correct, they were to protect me, not the flag.

I found Bonnie in the kitchen with Fred and Tigger, watching her put makeshift bandages on her arms. I'm sure Fred thought it was something delicious, but I knew Tigger was simply curious. She never seemed to be hungry, at least not while humans were present. "Did you get that calamine lotion, Jake?"

In the excitement of my epiphany, I'd completely spaced it out. "Uh, sorry. I forgot all about it when I realized who's been killing everyone. Do you want me to go back?"

Bonnie had been cradling her right arm like it had been blown off by a bomb and seemed to forget all about it and let it drop to her side. "You know who did it?" Her eyes were huge.

I felt the corners of my mouth form a smile. "Pretty sure, but I need to do a little experiment first."

She looked at the flag I'd carried in, then at me. Her facial expression changed faster than the Missouri weather. "Experiment? I hope it's not on Margot's flag. She'd kill us both if you do anything to it now that she knows what it's worth."

I wanted to say something about false hopes. For all we knew, the flag might not be worth a cent, but I let it go so I could get on with my experiment. "I don't have time to send it to a lab, so I'm going to experiment on myself. If I get the results I expect, I will know whodunit."

Bonnie went over to the cupboard where she kept her "medicine." "Would you stop talking in riddles, Jake, and tell me who did it." She was on her tiptoes, trying to reach the top cabinet. I had put her booze there at her request, so she'd have to get a stool to reach it. She was trying to cut down.

"Sit down. I'll get that for you and then I'll tell you all about my revelation."

To my surprise, she did as I'd asked and took a chair at the table facing me. Fred must have wanted to hear as well because he sat next to her. They looked like something Norman Rockwell would have painted for the *Saturday Evening Post*: an old lady with a broken arm and her dog looking sadly on. Tigger could have made the picture complete but got bored and went off searching for mice or whatever it is cats do when they tire of people.

I poured Bonnie her bourbon and sat down at the table opposite her. "I think Fitzgerald brushed up against the poison ivy in the caretaker's shed after stealing the flag from Captain Scott's grave. He must have given it to Amanda, who I suspect was to pass it on to Benson. Benson's not the collector of civil war artifacts as he claims. I think he's the fence. Anyway, when Fitzgerald died of his own stupidity, she must have thought Cramer killed him, and in turn, killed Cramer."

Bonnie refrained from taking her second sip to answer me. "But he was her father. She wouldn't kill her own father."

"Her *stepfather*, Bon. Bennett told me he abused her and her mother when she was a teenager. I have a feeling she hated him." My mind raced to finish. Most of what I was saying came to me as I spoke.

"Let me finish before you interrupt. I think she planted the flag in Kelly's hope chest in an attempt to frame her for the murder. I'll know for sure after I rub it on my good arm. It only took overnight before the rash showed up last time, so by morning we'll know if my theory is right."

Bonnie sat her glass down and frowned. "I still don't see how that proves anything, Jake."

I couldn't help suppress my grin. "I forgot to tell you that part. Amanda was scratching a rash on her arm the day I found the nosey neighbor in the barn."

I had a hard time sleeping. Even if Fred hadn't snored all night, I doubt if I could have slept. I wanted so much to expose Amanda so Kelly would be set free but didn't know how to do it. I could take what I knew to Bennett, but he'd laugh me all the way back to Colorado when I said it was because she'd caught poison ivy from a flag. Then there were all the loose ends. Why had she bought a sword and hidden it in the attic where she knew I'd find it eventually? Surely she knew I'd get around to fixing the insulation and have to start in the attic? And what was her motive for killing everyone in the first place? Bennett told me Cramer had abused her and her mother, but that was hearsay, and any smart lawyer would shoot that motive down in no time. It seemed the only way I could get Kelly released was if I got Amanda to confess. Maybe if I asked her nicely and said pretty please come clean, she'd do it. Sure. That was as realistic as Bonnie being canonized by the pope next week.

Morning finally came fifteen minutes after I'd fallen asleep. I knew it had to be morning because Fred was whining to be let out. I tried ignoring him by covering my head with a pillow, but he was smarter than me and pulled all of my blankets off. He must have known the cold air in the unheated sunroom would get me out of bed, and he was right. "Okay, Fred, you win," I said and stumbled out of bed. I dressed quickly and threw on my jacket while he watched me the way a fox watches a caged chicken.

Bonnie was sitting at the table when I passed through the kitchen on my way to the front door. "Afternoon, sunshine," she said.

I grunted something even I didn't understand

and let Fred out, then went back into the kitchen and poured myself a hot cup of coffee before sitting down to join her.

"Well?" she asked.

"Well, what?"

She twisted her mouth and spoke slowly like she was talking to a New York City taxi driver, fresh off the boat. "The...rash...Jake...Do you have poison ivy?"

I'd been so tired, I'd forgotten. I quickly looked at my arm. Except for a small cut where I'd lost a fight with a loose wrench working on the tractor several days ago, it was fine. "Maybe it's too soon," I said.

"Or maybe Amanda has psoriasis," she said, scooting her chair back. She rolled her eyes and went to the stove. "Scrambled okay? I don't have time to make a gourmet brunch today. The girls in my bible class invited me to a bridge game at noon in Lincoln."

"Fine, Bon, and thanks. I guess I better get back to that roof today. The snow should all be melted after yesterday's seventy-five degrees."

She turned, still holding an egg in her hand. By the look on her face, I was afraid she'd drop it. "You're not taking what you know to the sheriff?"

I shook my head before taking a deep breath. "No, Bon. I might have jumped the gun on that. The more I think about it, the more I realize Amanda's not our killer."

Bonnie smiled before turning back to the stove. "It'll be so nice to have a roof that doesn't leak. Maybe I'll be able to set up a sewing room in the spare bedroom."

Chapter 24

There was a time I could have laid fifteen squares of roofing and still finished in time to beat the rush-hour traffic home, but those days were long gone. By the time I'd finished loading the shingles, I was too tired to start nailing them down. I'd thought I'd been given a reprieve when Bonnie took off with her Jeep because I couldn't run into town for a ladder and hydraulic fluid. It turned out I couldn't use either of those reasons for an excuse to go back to bed. Cramer had a thirty-gallon drum of hydraulic fluid in the back of the barn and a stack of two by fours. I made a makeshift ladder with his two by fours and some nails he had in a coffee can on his workbench, and then topped off the fluid in the tractor using a hand pump that was attached to the top of the drum.

Fred and Tigger had followed me into the barn, but when it came time to load the shingles, they both disappeared. I didn't see them again until I'd finished and returned the tractor to the barn. "Where have you two been?" I asked after parking the tractor.

Fred didn't have time to answer, not that I really expected him to. I'd no sooner got off the tractor when it started to roll forward. It didn't have a parking brake, and I'd left it in neutral. Fred jumped out of the way, scaring Tigger, who took off for the loft.

"Of course, Fred. That's how they strung Cramer up there."

He tilted his head sideways. I expected him to say, "Huh," like Scooby Doo does when Shaggy questions him.

"The tractor, Fred. It must have rolled out of the way and the bucket lowered because of the leak. I've got to call the sheriff."

When Bennett didn't answer, I left him a message, telling him to meet me in the barn because I knew how Cramer had been strung up. I'd no sooner disconnected when I heard a car pull up. I only knew one person who drove an expensive Escalade. I was even more surprised to see Robin had come with her.

Fred ran over to Amanda. She bent down to pet him while Robin walked over to me.

"I hope we're not interrupting, Jake." She was out of uniform, so I guessed it was her day off.

"Not at all. I just finished loading the roof and was going to call it a day. Any news on Kelly?" I'd assumed it was why they had come. I couldn't imagine either one of them driving all the way out here just to chat with me.

Amanda and Fred joined us before Robin could answer. Fred ignored Robin and came over to sit by me.

"It's not looking good," Robin said, averting my eyes. "Chris is transferring her to Bolivar in the morning. Her lawyer has asked for a change in venue."

Amanda winced at the mention of her friend's name.

"Well, it's not often I get a visit from two good-looking women—what can I do for you?" I wanted to change the mood and didn't realize how stupid I sounded until I'd said it.

Robin didn't seem to notice, or maybe she simply chose to ignore my flattery. "We came to get Kelly's hope chest. She asked me if I'd take it back to my place for safe keeping. I couldn't fit it in my car, so I asked Amanda to help me."

I had no reason to doubt her, but something smelled like a backed-up septic tank. "Sure. It's back at the house. If you want to drive on over, I'll meet you there."

Amanda seemed to recover, no longer looking like she was attending a funeral. "Hop in, Jake. I'll give you a ride."

"Thanks, but I'll walk back with Fred."

I didn't really want to walk back to the house. It was a good hundred yards from the house, and I was dead tired after loading the roof, but I needed to make a phone call first.

Bonnie picked up on the on the first ring. "Bon, it's me, Jake."

"I know it's you, Jake. I have caller ID, remember?"

Ordinarily, I would have enjoyed our little banter and come back with a cute remark, but I had to make the call quick. "Are you still in Lincoln?"

"Yes. I'm just leaving the church. Why?"

"I need you to stop off at the so-called antique store for me and ask the kid who sold the sword for a description of his cougar."

"What? Oh, I see. You think it was Kelly he called a cougar. I knew it, Jake. I just knew it was her."

"Please, Bon, I don't have much time. Call me back as soon as you get a description." I had to get back before the women came looking for me, so I disconnected and hurried back to the house with Fred at my heels. I had no idea where Tigger had gone off to.

Amanda was sitting in one of the garage sale rockers Bonnie had bought recently. By the smile on her face, she seemed to be enjoying the soothing motion of the rocker. Robin was standing on the porch with her hands on her hips and a frown on her lips. Fred ran up to Amanda like he hadn't seen her in weeks. He kept his distance from Robin.

They'd backed the SUV up to the stairs and had the rear hatch open. A quick glance inside confirmed my suspicions—the cargo area was lined with blankets, the same pattern, and color as the ones in the tunnel.

"Sorry it took so long," I said, taking two steps at a time to reach the porch. "Come on in and I'll show you the chest."

Bonnie called back before I could open the door. "Please go on in; I need to get this."

Chapter 25

Both women were standing in the living room when I entered. Amanda was pointing at the rear of the house where I'd left the sunroom door open. I didn't bother to ask if she liked my decorating, led both women to the kitchen, and offered them chairs at the table. Fred went over to his bowl and slobbered water all over the floor.

Amanda took a chair, and Robin's eyes lit up when she saw the chest sitting by the pantry. She went straight to it, pulled a key from her purse, and opened it—she didn't look happy.

It was time to end the charade. "The reason I took so long is because I called Bennett and asked if he'd check with Kelly about the hope chest. That was him on the phone just now." It was a total fabrication. I figured if Robin had the day off, she wouldn't know if Bennett was in or not. They didn't need to know I lied. Not yet.

I carefully watched their faces. Amanda didn't

seem concerned and was rubbing Fred's head again. Robin stiffened and looked at me with an open mouth. Her eyes darted around the room before settling on me.

"Okay, Jake, I'll cut to the chase," she said, reaching under her sweatshirt for the gun she kept at her waist. "Give me the flag, and I promise not to shoot your dog."

Amanda looked like she'd given too much at the blood bank. Her face turned completely white, and she screamed. "What's going on, Robin?"

Fred started to growl.

Robin pointed her gun at him, and I used the distraction to move a few steps closer.

Robin smiled wickedly at Amanda. "You never were known for your brains, were you, Mandy. Why don't you just shut up and maybe I'll let you live? And hold that dog or he'll be the first to go."

Amanda grabbed Fred's collar just as he started to bare his teeth.

Satisfied, Robin turned to me. "Where'd I go wrong, Jake?"

"I started to suspect when you asked for the hope chest, but it wasn't until Bonnie called me back that I knew. The blankets in Amanda's car and the key confirmed it."

"What are you two talking about?" Amanda's

color was starting to come back.

"Robin's our murderer, and she framed Kelly."

Amanda's jaw dropped several inches. "Is this true, Robin?"

Robin laughed, bringing to mind the way the wicked witch in the *Wizard of Oz* had laughed. I expected to hear her say, "I'll get you, my pretty, and your little dog, too." Instead, she ignored Amanda and turned to me.

"Move any closer, Jake, and you'll look like Grace after I put a bullet in her head."

Then she turned toward Amanda but kept the gun pointed at me. "You're even dumber than Bobby thought. Of course, it's true."

Amanda's color was not only back, but she looked like her blood pressure was going to make her explode. "Bobby? You and Bobby?"

"I'm afraid so," I said, hoping she didn't do anything stupid and lash out at Robin.

Robin's smile returned, and she turned back to me. "When did you figure we were lovers, Jake?"

"When Bonnie told me it was you whom Jared called the cougar who bought the sword. That, and the fact you knew about the flag. You and Fitzgerald had to have been pretty close for him to tell you about it. Then it all fit. I couldn't for the life of me see why Amanda would buy the sword and hide it in her attic.

She had to know I'd find it when I started renovating the house."

Amanda almost let Fred go but grabbed him with her other hand before he attacked Robin. "Why would she buy it? If it was worth anything, wouldn't Bobby have given it to her to sell instead of hocking it?"

"Her prints were on it, Amanda. She had to get it before the sheriff did and sent it to Jefferson City. She knew it was the only thing that could connect her to Bobby and the grave robberies."

I turned to Robin. "Is that why you killed Cramer? Because he caught you snooping in the barn looking for the sword? Of course, you had no idea at the time Fitzgerald had already hocked it."

She pulled back the slide on her Glock, loading a round into the chamber. "You're too smart for your own good, Jake. I suppose now you're going to tell us how I managed to hang him from the rafters."

"That's the easy part."

Amanda looked at me wide-eyed.

"Ironically, she killed him in the cemetery."

Robin continued to smile. "How'd you know?"

"The tire tracks and a missing fence post, Robin. I assume you were taking him to the cemetery to shoot him when your gun jammed—the same gun, by the way, you later switched with Kelly's without her knowing" I took a deep breath and inched a bit closer.

"Cramer saw his chance to fight back after your gun jammed, so you picked up the next best thing to a gun and hit him with the fence post. I'm guessing that because you know something about forensic evidence, you didn't want to leave him where there were far too many of your footprints, so you decided to make it look like a suicide. That was when you got the tractor, hauled him into the barn, and hung him from the rafters. Your attempt to make it look like he'd hung himself was foiled by a leaky hydraulic system and an uneven floor. When the tractor rolled forward and the bucket lowered on its own after you left, there was no visible means for Cramer to have hung himself."

I paused to catch my breath while deciding if I was close enough to grab the gun. She waved me back, so I continued, "What I don't understand is why you killed the neighbors."

"What makes you think *I* killed them?"

"The bullet you sent to the lab in Jefferson City had no DNA on it. It couldn't possibly be the same bullet you removed from Grace's brain. I think you fired a bullet with Kelly's gun and sent that to the crime lab along with *her* gun."

She nodded her head and tightened her grip on the gun. "Well, I guess it won't hurt to tell you before

I shoot you. Like they say, dead men tell no tales. He caught me in the barn. I'd come back looking for the Captain's battle flag when I saw one like it sold for nearly a million dollars. That kind of money would be more than enough to get me out of this cow town." She paused for a moment before continuing, probably to imagine how she'd spend all that money. She didn't notice Tigger coming through the kitty door.

"I'd found the flag in a hope chest at the back of the barn with a Bowie knife laying on top of it. I'd just picked up the knife when I heard the click of a gun hammer behind me. I turned around with the knife behind my back to see the nosy neighbor, pointing a shotgun in my face. The idiot put it too close to me and I was able to knock it out of his hand with one hand and stab him in the chest with the other. Unfortunately, the gun went off before he hit the ground. I knew who he was and knew where he lived. I couldn't take the chance his girlfriend heard the gun, so I drove his truck over to their house and shot her in the head when she opened the door. I was too scared to go back for the flag and left. I had to wait until now to come back. I couldn't take the chance one of our deputies, or your dog would catch me in the barn. Then I got the idea to bring Amanda along on the pretense Kelly had sent us."

Her smile was gone. She put both hands on her

gun and aimed it at my head. "Bye, Jake. I wish you hadn't been so clever."

Amanda screamed and let Fred loose at the same time Tigger decided to join us and jump up on the table. It didn't stop Robin from firing, but Tigger distracted her enough that she missed when I rushed in to grab her arm. I had her on the ground in a split second, but she still had the gun in her hand. Fred didn't have enough sense to be afraid she might shoot and sunk his teeth into her hand, causing the gun to go off at the same time Bennett busted in the front door. Everything happened so fast. It seems Bennett got my message or Bonnie had called him. Either way, it was too late for my best friend—Fred was lying still on the floor in a pool of blood.

Chapter 26

Bonnie couldn't stop crying while we sat in the waiting room. I had rushed Fred to the vet's without waiting for Bennett to arrest Robin. I'd thought I'd lost Fred, but when he raised his head and looked at me with the saddest eyes I'd ever seen, I grabbed him and broke all speeding laws to get him to the vet.

He'd been in surgery for over an hour when the front door opened and Kelly walked in. She came straight over to me and hugged me. "Chris told me what happened. Is Fred going to be okay?" Her eyes were red with tears.

I should have asked if she was a free woman now that Robin had been arrested, but I couldn't talk because I was afraid I'd start to cry. Grown men don't cry, my father had always said. Luckily the vet chose that moment to bring us up to date on Fred's condition.

"He's one lucky dog, Mr. Martin. The bullet nicked an artery and missed his spleen by an inch. He should be good as new in a few days."

Bonnie started bawling, and I could see it wouldn't take much before Kelly did, too.

"Thank you, doctor. I really don't know what I'd do without him. He's all I have."

Kelly hugged me again. "Not if I have anything to say about it, Jake. I've waited all my life for someone like you, and I'm not going to let you get away that easily."

I waited for her to release me from her hug, then took her head in my hands and kissed her.

About the Author

Richard Houston is a retired software engineer who now lives on Lake of The Ozarks with a view to die for. He and his wife are raising their great-granddaughter, two Dachshunds, and a Golden Retriever.

If you enjoyed this book, please leave a review, and be sure to check out the others in the series:

A View to Die For

A Book to Die For

A Treasure to Die For

Letters to Die For

Books to Die For, A boxed set of the first three books

Visit him at

http://houstonrichard.wixsite.com/books

Made in the USA
Middletown, DE
28 October 2018